ONE MAN'S LOSS

Sir Christian Leigh-Bolton had never intended to gamble that night the vultures circled around Sir Howard. Losing heavily and in desperation, Sir Howard foolishly wagers away his inheritance, Kingsley Hall — and Christian steps in and wins the prize. Sir Howard's actions leave his sister, Eleanor, virtually homeless. Christian's honour is further tested when he makes a promise to Sir Howard, a dying man, not knowing if he can fulfil it. Meanwhile, Eleanor has taken matters into her own hands . . .

VALERIE HOLMES

◆

ONE MAN'S LOSS

Complete and Unabridged

LINFORD
Leicester

First published in Great Britain in 2021

First Linford Edition
published 2021

A catalogue record for this book is available
from the British Library.

ISBN 978–1–4448–4637–9

Published by
Ulverscroft Limited
Anstey, Leicestershire

Set by Words & Graphics Ltd.
Anstey, Leicestershire
Printed and bound in Great Britain by
TJ Books Ltd., Padstow, Cornwall

This book is printed on acid-free paper

1

Eleanor approached the grand terraced house with a heavy heart masked by a pleasant expression on her face. She tried to scrape the mud off her boots before lifting the heavy door knocker and waited to be allowed inside. Taking a minute to even out her breathing, she glanced back down the avenue.

The day was sunny enough, but she had walked for nearly two hours, no coach to spare her the detritus of the streets. Mrs Minerve Jennings, her mother's old companion, had warned her she was on a fool's errand. Yet Eleanor could not believe this desperate situation. These people were of her blood only through her uncle — but still, she reasoned, family was family! Aunt Amelia would be only too pleased to welcome her into the lovely spacious family home; just as she had four

Christmastides ago, when Eleanor's circumstances had been so very different . . . wouldn't she?

The highly polished black door opened, revealing the familiar black-and-white chequered tiled floor of the immaculate entrance hall inside.

'My card,' Eleanor said, offering it to the young maid who stared at her, then glanced behind the visitor with a bemused expression at the absence of a chaperone or carriage. She stared at her lone figure, then stepped aside and showed her into the entrance hall, where Eleanor paused, marvelling at the contrast of the floor against the white of the plastered walls. Memories of flickering candlesticks, bright green-and-red holly, mistletoe garlands and music filling the hallway, along with the distinctive smell of citrus fruits and spices, flooded back to fill her dulled senses. Eleanor smiled, relieved to be here, remembering fondly the welcoming warming glass of mulled wine as the guests had entered this sheltered, privileged world.

She watched the girl place her card on a small silver tray that had been left on the hallway table for this purpose, and then skip easily up the sweeping carpeted stairs. Eleanor watched, admiring her energy. Her eyes took in the grandeur of the Grecian columns that lined the side of this magnificent entrance. Her own home, Kinsley Hall — or, rather, the place that until recently had been her home — was just as grand, but it originated from an earlier period in history. Unlike this bright interior, the oak that lined its walls had darkened over the years; magnificent, but in stark contrast to this new building. However, Eleanor knew she would soon adjust to it, she had no doubt of that. The weight began to lift from her shoulders and she took a moment to breathe more easily, away from the stench of the road and the noise of vendors touting their trades. Her life would not be the same, but here at least it could continue as it should.

The door upstairs was opened as her aunt's voice resonated off the hard walls. 'I am not in, Ida, tell her that I am not in!' the lady of the house ordered the maid.

Eleanor's gloved hand flew to her mouth to stop a sob of disbelief escaping as the words echoed in her unbelieving head.

'Tell her I have gone away with her cousin Harriet, and we do not expect to return before the Season.' The door was closed. The words had clearly been meant to carry down the stairwell so that she would be in no doubt the woman meant them.

The even more bemused maid ran back down the stairs to deliver the brusque message, but Miss Eleanor Richards had heard the dismissal loud and clear and duly turned around, leaving of her own accord before she was humiliated further by the delivery of her aunt's cold rebuff.

Outside in the street, Eleanor glanced

4

up and saw the curtain in the upstairs morning room flicker. Her only aunt, the widow of her dear father's brother, had made her stance on Eleanor's unfortunate position clear. She was as a social outcast! Eleanor swallowed back the tears that were rising, threatening to cascade down her already cold, pale cheeks. She could be homeless and destitute as far as that woman was concerned, her prospects reduced to being valued as nil in society.

Eleanor tilted her head back, breathing deeply, whilst looking out from under her bonnet's brim, and walked off towards the Minster. York had always been a favourite place of hers and her brother's. However, now he had gone to be with God the Father of the grand cathedral, leaving his wife Jemima and her baby boy to inherit Kinsley Hall. What irked Eleanor grievously was that Jemima hated Kinsley as much as she did Eleanor's native Yorkshire. The woman had even kept Howard's death to herself for a whole week whilst she planned her next move. Then she calmly arrived at breakfast dressed in a widow's garb, telling Eleanor that Howard had died a hero; that the Hall was to be sold, and Jemima and her son would return to her family home in Kent. Arrangements had been made to take the Kinsley coach back to her own relatives, where they would live with her cousin Edward in the equally grand town of Tonbridge Wells. Sigmund, her son, would be her cousin's heir as he had none, having never married. Leaving Eleanor at the mercy of her only relative, her aunt — or so Jemima thought. It had been made more than clear to Eleanor that her presence in Kent would present an extra burden that would be impossible for Jemima's cousin to bear. Within two months of the news of Howard's death, still wearing mourning, Eleanor was being made homeless.

With only a few pounds between her and destitution, along with her own meagre possessions rescued from the

Hall — those she could carry — she was to be seen as a gentle lady fallen on diminished circumstances. Jemima had been given Eleanor's mother's jewels by Howard, except for a ruby necklace that he had not known about. That was not all, though. There were other small gifts, some quite valuable ones, that Eleanor's mother had told her to take should her daughter ever need them after her own passing. It had been hard to listen to the woman's wise words, but she had obviously seen what could happen when Jemima arrived as Howard's new wife. They had been married in France, Jemima the young widow of Howard's fallen Captain, who had found herself in an awkward situation, Howard had stepped in and honourably helped her, or so the woman claimed. That was the past; how Eleanor accessed these other maternal gifts now was a mystery she had yet to solve.

Eleanor's feet already ached. She had walked for more than two hours to reach this grand address; now she must return to the only friend she apparently had left who would help her. Turning down a small alley, she stopped by the back of an inn where deliveries were being made.

It had been a wild hope that he was still there. Fortune, it appeared, was at least providing her with some good for a change.

'Samuel Higgs, isn't it?' she asked, as if she did not know who the son of the dairy farm on the estate was. By sheer chance she had seen him pull up to turn his wagon behind the inn, but had not wanted to be seen walking the streets on her own, and so had dashed down a snicket to avoid embarrassment. Now her joy was hard to contain as she saw him readying his empty wagon to return to the estate. How quickly things changed, she thought, as she watched the recognition dawn across his face.

'Aye, miss,' he said. The cart was empty and the horse was hitched and ready.

'I wondered if you would do me a kindness,' Eleanor said, and tried not to sound as desperate as she felt.

'If it's in me power to do so, miss, then aye, of course.' He tilted his head to one side, curious. She tried to subdue an urge to smile because momentarily he reminded her of her father's old cocker spaniel that he owned when she was just a child. What a lovely time that had been in her life.

'I wondered if . . . well, you are returning home, are you not?' She tried not to lose her confidence as the light would fade soon, and she had no wish to be found on the streets of the city after dark.

'Are you wanting a lift, miss?' he said quietly to her. 'Is that it?'

'If you would not mind, Samuel.' She let out the breath she had been holding and nodded back. He instantly jumped down and helped her up to sit next to him on the front seat of the wagon. He touched his flat cap as a mark of respect, even though this was all highly

9

irregular. If her aunt could see her now she would call her wanton. But Eleanor could hardly walk the city streets alone as night crept over the city like a dark and ominous blanket.

'It's no bother, miss. You'll be more comfortable and cleaner sat up here with me, miss.' Then he added, 'We all feel your loss and, well, if it's Minnie's you be heading to, I reckon I can pass by her door. Her cottage is quite hidden, miss, so no one need know. It's deep in them old woods.' He winked at her — kindly, not mockingly. Eleanor could not help but wonder how many of her father's long-serving estate workers knew the truth of her situation.

'Splendid! Thank you, Samuel,' she said, hoping if anyone who knew her from her normal round of acquaintances saw her from their fine carriages leaving the city on a wagon with a farm worker, they would not realise who she was. Then she frowned as one undeniable thought struck her — what if they did? Carriages were hardly lining up to whisk her away to share their respect-able homes. However, they were few anyway, which gave her some peace of mind.

'You worry none, miss. Good will win out.' Samuel climbed up next to her; at least he seemed genuinely pleased to have her company.

She smiled back. How could he understand? Yet she blinked, because what did she know or understand about his daily life — the wars, or the impact of losing the only provider in the household on foreign soil? His father had perished five years previ-ously and Samuel had since taken over the farm. Perhaps they had more in common now than before. Words failed her as she contemplated the humble door that she had to knock on next. *Humility, Ellie*, she silently remon-strated. She had to be grateful for small mercies and kindly folk like Minnie and Samuel.

Eleanor was helped down outside the gate to Mrs Jennings' cottage. At least here she would be welcomed, but the shame she felt to have to be grateful for it made her cheeks burn. Hatred was a strong word, but what Jemima had done to her made her wish the woman ill. Yet that too was unkind, for did she not have a lovely innocent child dependent upon her? *Oh* . . . Tears welled; she would never see Sigmund's little face again.

Eleanor balled her fists. She would not succumb to blubbering. She needed her wits about her to stay strong. Yes, she had been brought low; but, by all that was sacred to the memory of her dear mother, she would be strong. Eleanor's hard-working, blinkered father had never seen the flaws in his son's nature: her soft-hearted and possibly stupid brother's desire for pleasure over hard graft. Howard had the business acumen of a laundry maid, but not their work ethic. Eleanor would survive and come back in force, and Jemima would eat humble pie at Eleanor's table. It would not be revenge, but she would see justice done.

First, though, she had to survive!

2

'No luck, my dear?' Mrs Jennings — Minnie, as Eleanor's mother had affectionately called her — said before ushering her inside the cottage, taking her bonnet and pelisse. Candles flickered and an oil lamp glowed from a small adjacent room. It was small to Eleanor compared to the spacious rooms of Kinsley Hall.

Eleanor shook her head. She did not want the woman to gloat even if she had every right to.

'Told you, lass, eh; your type of folk run a mile from scandal, and, well, young Howard died in . . . unclear circumstances, and lost his inheritance into the bargain.' She coughed. 'Now, you come through to me cosy kitchen, we don't want gossip on the doorstep now, do we?' She laughed, knowing there was no one for half a mile. Unless

Samuel talked to more than the cows on his farm, Eleanor's present whereabouts would remain fairly unknown. The short, rotund, apron-clad woman looked up the garden path with squinted eyes — evening had closed in on them — as if the birds and trees were listening to her.

Eleanor could not bear it any more. She had loved Howard, and could never see what had attracted him to the venomous bitch he married. What were the 'unclear circumstances' Mrs Jennings referred to? Jemima had told her that he died a hero, yet no details were given to her as to how so. That did not explain how Kinsley Hall had been transferred to a total stranger. She had never even read the letter that the solicitor delivered personally to Jemima. Eleanor had seen him arrive, but unknowing as to what his business was, she had passed the time of day politely with him until her sister-in-law was free, and yet he never even hinted that he brought such dire news.

'There is no scandal in a man dying too soon, Minnie!' Eleanor said, using the familiar name her mother would have.

'Well, the war's finished and he must have been one of the last to go there and to fall, unlucky blighter. Pardon me, but when luck was shared out they missed his cup, lass.' She coughed. 'Also, to gamble away the estate! Lass, he was no hero. Anyways, come on, Ellie, can't have you standing here freezing like.'

Eleanor thought *Touché!* as the woman had answered her in kind. No one but Howard had called her Ellie since her mama died five summers previously.

She hesitated, wondering what she would do now if this kindly woman also turned against her; patience and tolerance would need to be her watchwords until she could remove herself to a more respectable place and finer living.

Following Mrs Jennings' lead for the time being seemed the sensible thing to do. She did not want to sit in a small bedroom, in a city inn, on her own with no maid, wasting away with worry as to what she would or could do next. With no prospects or chaperone, she would hardly attract a decent marriage proposal.

Eleanor had never worked a day in her life, and it showed. Why should she have? As the lady of the house — until her brother married the witch, that is — it had not been needed. She had been tended by their servants. What could she do, anyway, other than teach the things she already knew to children? How would she obtain a governess's position without a reference or an introduction? The thought of it made her pale: living as a shadow figure between the family and staff — a life of isolation, except for her wards. It did not appeal to her at all.

'Lass, come on and have a tot of brandy in me kitchen, whilst I rustle up some batter pudding and ham from me larder. Don't look around at me home

17

like that, it don't do to look a gift horse in the mouth — so to speak. You look like tha's lost, but this cottage is plenty big enough for us two. The Hendersons had eight under its roof and they thought it a fine place to live. Crikey, whole families live in one-room cottages on the estate, so this is like a palace!' She chuckled.

Eleanor did not. She stared at the narrow hall, the low roof and roughly plastered walls.

'Look, Ellie, you have been spared from total ruin and starvation, so smile. If you reject me kitchen's offerings and me back room for a place to kip, then the streets is a far lonelier and colder place; especially for a fine lady like you. Your pa would have been rocked to the core if he had known that folk in your family had gone and left you like this — all alone.'

'That sort of thought is not going to help me now, is it?' Eleanor snapped out her words, but her eyes were watering and she swallowed hard. She was so hungry and tired; ashamedly, the tears were now ready to flow.

'Yes, well, I'll forgive that remark because you're damned right! Now, none of that snivelling here — no blubbering!' Minnie stepped back and let Eleanor pass her by in the narrow passage. Three rooms led off it: a front parlour, a bedroom and a back kitchen beyond that. 'Your ma was a fighter and I loved that woman dearly. Now, you dry those eyes of yours, and after you've fed and rested we shall set them on a clear course, where things will look much better. You have just Minnie between a fed belly and a warm bed, and the dirty cold street — your choice, lass!' She raised both eyebrows but Eleanor passed by her without a word whilst she breathed in her tears and swallowed deep. The woman was not sparing with her simple home truths.

'I'm sorry, Mrs Jennings, I did not mean to be disingenuous.' She wiped her eyes with the back of her gloved hand.

'Good, 'cause you are a good lass and I'll help thee, but you are going to have to live my life as is, as I cannot climb that ladder to reach the one you have . . . had. So are you going to stay put, or risk spending your last shilling begging at the door of another family member or 'friend'?' Minnie shut the door firmly and bolted it behind her. No answer was expected.

'No, that I am not. I will not beg at any more doors. They are firmly shut against me, Minnie — other than yours, of course, which I am most grateful for. Mother trusted you and loved you dearly, and I shall be honoured to stay here. Perhaps I can pay you a small rent, or . . . ' Eleanor had no idea what else she could offer. There was no way that she was prepared to sell her mother's rubies if she could avoid it. For one thing, if she did so too soon and word managed to reach Jemima, Eleanor wondered if she could accuse her of being a thief. And how would she be able to bargain a fair price for something that to her was priceless? How would she know what they were worth, or how to sell them even if she wished to — which she did not.

So she would survive until time and distance was placed between her and the sister-in-law she had begun to hate; a strong emotion that Eleanor had never known she possessed. Yet somehow she must manage in the meantime. Minnie was her best, if not her only, hope. If she was to remain respectable, out of sight, and stand a chance of regaining some of the lifestyle she had been born to, then she needed a safe place to live and at some point regain access to the Hall. There were things there that were hers by right, some had value and she must retrieve them. How though? That would be a question she would answer once she had eaten and rested. There was no way she could ask her aunt for help in the matter, so a different kind of plan had to form.

Aunt Amelia had firmly closed the door on the possibility of an official family visit to the Hall to make a plea of conscience, respectably, to the new owner, whoever they might be.

'Oh no, lass, you'll not pay me a farthing. You are not to be me mistress or me lodger. You stay here as a friend or my companion, but you help Minnie when asked, and I will show you how to live happily again — or at least contentedly, and that is more than many ever manage. How to enjoy the good health you have and put all this sadness behind you. But when I do ask you to do something for me, you do it without question — agreed?' Minnie bobbed her head to stress her words whilst her cloth bonnet flopped against her wiry greying hair.

'How to live?' Eleanor looked at her, mystified. What was the woman asking her to agree to do? She wanted to trust Minnie, but she felt like she could be in the jaws of a trap. To give her word of obedience and then renege on it was unthinkable. She was a lady who had mixed in the limited society of the county — yet had been excluded from it because of the circumstances surrounding Howard's death. The world loved a gambler when they were successful, but disowned one who was a loser, it appeared; but at the same time, she knew so little of Minnie's life.

'Yes, survive, and learn to live a very different wholesome life, find a respectable way through the mire — because, my dear Eleanor, you have been left knee-deep in one that would not look out of place in a pigsty. So dry them eyes and come and have a natter with Minnie, and a brandy with some food on me kitchen table, and see how the other 'alf live. For them folks on the street back in yonder city out there are dying, love. There is no work for returnees from the wars. So look on my humble fare with a kindly and grateful eye.'

Eleanor sat on the rickety chair by the small range and sipped brandy from an old chipped porcelain cup that she recognised from her mother's old set back from when she was a child.

Minnie nestled into her own comfy chair after placing a plate with a large slice of Yorkshire pudding and Yorkshire ham on top of the range, as the gravy warmed in a pan with leftover turnip from the woman's meal from the day before. 'It'll be ready soon; you sip that and drink it down good, lass. You've been walking around York most the day, haven't you, trying to pluck up courage to come back to Minnie's door?' The woman shook her head. 'You should have come here sooner. I don't bear grudges against them that did me no wrong.' She took a sip of her own drink and slapped her lips together. 'Tommy provides some good stuff, you know.' She shook her head and added quietly, 'Or perhaps you don't.'

Eleanor agreed. She felt the brandy dull her senses, coupled with the comfort of the heat from the range; whilst nestling in the old chair made her feel strangely relaxed, almost sleepy if she had not been so hungry. She could hardly deny Minnie's blunt observations; she had been wronged by Eleanor's family, but then so had Eleanor.

Gazing blankly around this small room with its crooked table, small range and these two worn-out chairs taking up most of the space, Eleanor could never have envisaged living like this and being remotely grateful for the chance. Yet that was both unkind and cruel because Minnie had not hesitated to share the little she had in the world with her. Next to Eleanor was the only cupboard, housing the larder; she could see this as there was a split between the panels of the old oak door.

A strange sensation swept through her of feeling both lost and found at the same time. Happy and sad, for she was being cared for — but not by her only nearby relative, who could have lifted her station higher than it had been before Howard's death; taken her in as the woman's ward, or at the very least a much-loved companion.

This place was claustrophobic compared to the high ceilings, spacious lounges and day rooms of Kinsley Hall, yet it was strangely comforting — or was that the effect of the brandy? Like a cocoon protecting her from the squalor and detritus on the streets of the city that awaited those fallen from the grace of wealth, to share this home with a familiar face, her mother's lifelong companion, who her brother and his wife had terminated the services of immediately the day her mother died. Fortunately, at least she had been left a stipend from the estate that Jemima and Edward could not touch, or she too would have been out on the street. Coming here had not been easy because of the shame Eleanor felt for the way Minnie had been dismissed. If only her mother had left Eleanor something independently, her own cottage, but she had trusted Howard implicitly to care for his sister.

Minnie had, on her own instigation, opened her door and her heart to

Eleanor, and that meant a lot, so she smiled politely back at the woman.

'Ah, that's better. It's amazing how a tot of brandy can clear a person's vision. You shall be as me own lost daughter — aye — that's it! If I'd been blessed with one, that is.' She nodded.

With the drink and the appetising smell of the warming food on the range, Eleanor fought the urge to sleep; she was re-awoken from her stupor when the harsh dismissal of her aunt's words resounded in her head. Society's door had closed and Eleanor was on the wrong side of it. Yet here, instead of being desolate and cold, she was warm; and, as she ate, her happier childhood memories flooded back. Yes, she would do well here. She would learn to live.

'Thank you, Minnie.'

'Aye, lass, thank *you*; for I am sorely in need of some good company and a steady hand that can sew. So feel free to butter me up, lass.' Minnie winked and chuckled.

Eleanor felt no menace in the

woman, but this time smiled back somewhat tentatively.

3

Sir Christian Leigh-Bolton arrived at Kinsley Hall in the dead of night. Fortunately the housekeeper, Mrs Hitchins, must have waited up for him, or so he thought as an oil lamp flickered in a downstairs window. He had the key; it was heavy enough to anchor a man-of-war, he had bemoaned, when he had been unceremoniously presented with it along with the deeds in the offices of Bellingham and Crouch, of Baxtergate, York.

'Good God!' he exclaimed as he entered the dark depths of the hallway, placing his tall hat on the stand, along with the key. He did not see why he should have to slam the old iron-headed door knocker down hard to gain entry into his own home.

The ancient panelled walls made the

place appear gloomy like his mood. *They will have to go!* he promised himself, as he preferred a lighter ambiance to a home rather than one that reminded him of a funeral pyre waiting to be set light to; a cage of aged wood.

He continued straight into what was obviously the library; he had seen the plans, and felt at least as though he knew where rooms were located. He looked sadly upon the fire that dwindled in the hearth; it seemed to have lost the will to survive. The lamp was also succumbing to the dark of the night. He loosened his greatcoat and rubbed his hands together. Someone would have to see to his horse, for it also needed caring for. Where was the damned woman?

'Sorry, sir . . . ' A flustered Mrs Hitchins scurried by past him without stopping as she made for the fire to poke and rekindle the dying flames.

'Sorry, sir,' she repeated, 'I nodded off in the chair. You must have been very long in the saddle,' she said, obviously very tired and her wits apparently still half in sleep. 'I was sent word that you would be delayed as your uncle had taken ill,' she continued, standing straight again. Stifling a yawn, she added, 'But didn't think you'd arrive this late . . . '

'Well, he died.' Even to Christian his words sounded as cold as this insufferably long night had been. 'Please wake the cook from her bed and tell her that I need something hot to eat — and soon, before I join my uncle! Then get the stable hand to see to my horse. It has brought me a long way and needs tending to.' His words were snapped out like orders: he was not in the army any more, but such habits were hard to break, especially when you were cold, hungry and tired.

If the damnable coach had not lost a wheel somewhere between Selby and York he would have at least arrived in some warmth. The woman hesitated, looking near to tears as she stood before him in her night robe, shawl, slippers and cap. She had not stayed up; of course she wouldn't, he had not been expected to arrive in the dead of night. Damnation, he had pounded on the door fit to wake the dead as he unlocked it and flung it open. What a first impression to make upon his new staff!

'Just ask her for a plate of food, cold if it must be and a glass of her best brandy.' He tried to look pleasant now that his face was not so frozen and was regaining some of its normal animation.

'I cannot, sir. You see, there is no cook.' The woman took a step backwards when he spun around to face her; his attention had been on the fire where he was warming his hands and enjoying feeling the colour return to his cheeks.

'You jest, surely!' he said, but could plainly see by her wan pallor in the limited light of the lamp she was carrying that she did not.

'I was waiting on word, Sir Leigh-B —'

'Sir, will do . . .'

'Sir, I was waiting for your instructions. But there was no communication and so I could not stop people leaving.' She swallowed.

'I am supposed to be taking over the Hall, estate, fishing rights, tenants and staff.' He stood straight, suspecting that all was not as he expected it to be.

'Well, the Hall is as it is — in good order. The tenants are anxiously waiting for you to tell them what is happening under your ownership — the estate manager left, sir, when Master Howard's wife fired him. That was the day before she too left the estate. The staff is much reduced. I know nothing of the fish- . . .' Her voice trailed off.

Christian detected a trace of sarcasm until he raised one dark eyebrow, staring blankly back even if it was hardly the woman's fault. He had been duped, it appeared. The lowlife cad,

Howard, had sold him the Kinsley estate in its entirety, yet had ordered his soon-to-be widow to diminish it further before she too left.

The circumstances of the transfer of Kinsley were mainly due to Sir Howard's ruinous gambling. The sale furnished a vast debt owed to Christian, which was created by Howard's hedonistic lifestyle. Ultimately the man had ruined his health prematurely — he was a rank coward anyway. That aside, the estate was supposed to have been fully staffed, but like a fool Christian had not ascertained by how many servants.

'Well most of the staff were stood down, by instruction of Sir Howard, the Hall's master, through his widow, before he died, sir. Everyone presumed it was at your request . . . ' Her lips clenched into a thin line.

'So how many staff am I blessed with?' He realised this woman had much pent-up anger and would love to vent it at him, but dared not, rightly so.

The woman shifted uneasily. 'Well,

sir, counting myself, four. The game-keeper, Tommy Squires, lives on the estate and has been trying to keep the place together, and then there are two maids, Annie and Florrie, one upper, one kitchen/laundry.' She cleared her throat. 'Together we've kept the place in order for the past month, sir, since Lady Jemima left.'

'Can you trace any of the original staff that worked here before?' he asked.

'I think so, but some will have taken new positions . . . in York, or on the manor houses roundabout here . . . like I have also done, sir.' She tipped her head up slightly, bracing herself for his response to this admission.

'What!' he snapped at her, and she flinched, taking a step backward.

'Yes, sir, I must leave in two weeks' time. I cannot survive without any payment for my services, even if your intentions were to make up the arrears. Besides, the lady of the house gave me an excellent reference and recommended a physician's household in York before she too left. She was lovely, so beautiful, and it was so wrong what happened to her . . . Oh, poor Miss Eleanor . . . ' Her hand shot to her mouth.

'Damnation! The lady should not have married a drunken buffoon, then!' He shouted the words out and buttoned up his coat again; he would have to see to the horse himself.

'Not that lady . . . '

'Quiet, woman! I have heard quite enough for one night.'

She walked away briskly before Christian could call her back, and then ran from the room.

Once his ex-sergeant Bill Raynor arrived with the mended coach, he would send the man back to York with the animal. His mood instantly mellowed, as it would be good to have Bill back; there was work to do here, even in the dark he could tell that. If the household was so diminished, then he needed his friend watching . . . ear to the ground.

With a humongous effort he strode away from the warmth of the fireside, making his way through to the kitchens. Once Annie, the young maid, had stopped screaming — he had burst into her room behind the wall that housed the kitchen's main range — he managed to get her to realise he was the new master of the Hall and not an intruder. This must be the warmest room in the house, he thought.

'Calm down, girl, or one of us will have a fainting fit, and I don't think it will be me. I am the owner of this estate and I need food,' he said as calmly as he could, as she clung to her shawl as if he were going to rip it from her and ravage her.

Once her snivelling had stopped he set her to making him hot chocolate, eggs, ham and warmed bread whilst he saw to the horse. By the time he was chilled to the bone again he returned to the kitchen, where his supper had been left on the table laid out for him. The girl had returned to her room, door shut firmly. He had no wish to find out whether it was locked or not. It was food he wanted, not to scare a young maid out of her wits.

Christian ate, drank and fell asleep slumped over the table, his plate pushed to the side. When he awoke with a stiff neck, he straightened up. Dawn was near breaking so he made his way up to the master bedroom at the centre of the upper landing and fell on the bed. Sleep came to him easily.

He only stirred when he heard the wheels of a coach churning up the gravel on the drive below.

'Ah! Bill, my man, now we can begin!' Christian was instantly awake, like any good soldier who had served and stood watch in the night. He descended the stairs two at a time and was calmly standing in the hall when the door was pushed open and his old sergeant stood beaming before him.

'Not a bad dive is it, sir?' he said, nodding to the walls around him, then added, 'You look like sh . . . Morning, ma'am . . . ' Bill shone a friendly smile at Mrs Hitchins, who, now fully and immaculately dressed, had appeared from the dining room.

'Your breakfast will be served shortly, sir,' she said to Christian. 'Should I have Annie rustle up something for your . . . man?' Her voice trailed off with a lack of enthusiasm.

Christian withheld his urge to grin, reading the annoyance in Bill's eyes, despite his impassive face. His man was very proud to have served with Christian, and had no time for pompous wenches who thought themselves better than a worker.

'Yes, Mrs Hitchins, as he has to return with the horse to the city, once he has eaten and has seen to the coach.' With his back to Mrs Hitchins, who left them alone, Christian grinned at Bill and walked to the doorway to greet him properly.

'I could've returned to me brother in London, you know. I didn't have to come all the way up here to no man's land to be slighted by a witch hiding in plain sight.' Bill's gruff voice was low, but Christian knew that the man's brother was an alcoholic and lived in the Isle of Dogs, so that would be the last place Bill, a teetotaller by choice, would take refuge.

'She is harmless, I suspect. Anyway, she is not staying. Bill, I need you to find out where the other servants are — we need them back. Chat to the girl, Annie, in the kitchen. She has been left to be maid of all in a place this size, with only one upstairs to help out. Be gentle with her, she nearly had heart failure when I burst in last night. See if she can help. There's a gamekeeper who's been running the estate in the void — find out what he is like. Also what he's been stealing or doing whilst he has had free rein to act as the lord of the manor. Lest he's a saint and as straight as an arrow, then make sure he has no intention of leaving!' Christian whispered his orders to the man, who raised quizzical eyebrows in return to the last comment.

'Yes, sir.' He stepped away.

'Bill,' Christian said. 'Good to have you here!'

The man did not turn back, but chuckled. 'Aye, well, sir, like you said, where the hell else would I be?'

4

Christian ate his breakfast, which was hearty enough to set him up for a good ride around the estate. The meal had been basic in content, but freshly cooked, certainly better than Christian had put up with for his meals when they were on campaigns; a lot better than army fare! Bill would have been greatly offended by the idea, as he thought himself to be a better cook than he actually was. However, Christian knew that his resourceful sergeant had put many a half-decent meal on his plate when supplies were short in camp. His men had not been so fortunate.

'Mrs Hitchins!' he shouted as he left the dining room. If that woman smiled, he thought, her face might actually crack like a limestone pavement. He would not miss her presence once she had run away from what she obviously thought was a sinking ship, but that was her loss. She reminded him of a strict governess he had once been blessed with who he could never please. He had had several such in his younger days, all handy with a cane, and all who he had despised. He smiled to himself; he had done little to please any of them, and given each a hard time. Although, since becoming a man, one sobering thought had haunted him — for how would a boy have known that, for a single woman of good family to be dismissed from a governess's position, it could force them into a more desperate life?

'Yes, sir?' Mrs Hitchins broke his moment of reflection and appeared from the morning room like an apparition of doom, with heavy grey dress, hair tied in a severely pulled-back grizzled grey bun, wearing highly polished black boots clanking on the tiles as she approached. A chain with keys hanging from it hung from a black leather belt, reminding him of an ancient Saxon lady holding the keys to the great hall, or perhaps more befittingly the demeanour of a modern asylum nurse — no, that was too harsh, she was not hard or cruel enough for that. With her hands holding each other at waist height she stood posed in front of him.

Christian may have arrived at an odd hour of the morning, and it may have been inconsiderate and his mood boorish, but he was not about to apologise to a house servant because his arrangements had gone awry, and certainly not to one who looked down upon his sergeant.

'Ah, Mrs Hitchins, there you are. Do you know where I can find a good cook who either lives nearby or would be prepared to leave the city for a decent living, with immediate effect?' First things first, he mused. 'And, of course, where I can find a replacement for you?' he added, and saw her disapproval of the order of his priorities.

'There are agencies in York, though they will take time to make a suitable

44

selection — but then good staff are in high demand, especially housekeepers . . . and cooks.' Her nose seemed to tilt upwards as she mentioned her own role. 'However, if you want a woman who would make an excellent house-keeper and who is also a more than passable good country cook, rather than a fancy one who you could hire in if needed for soirees and balls, then there is a lady who lives on the estate who may help you out. She used to be a companion for the elder lady of the Hall, prior to Mr Howard's possession of it. She also covered for the then-cook, when she was too busy elsewhere. Her name is Mrs Minerve Jennings, and she lives at Briar Cottage; it was bequeathed her until the day she . . . until she no longer needs it, sir.' She sniffed.

'Until she's dead, you mean?' Christian regretted his direct response as soon as the words hit the woman's ashen face. God, he had been a soldier far too long! She clearly knew this

Jennings woman well enough, regarded her highly, and, as an uptight sensitive soul who could not bear to hear the harsh realities of life spoken out loud, she was offended by his manner again.

'Yes! That is precisely what I meant.' Her words snapped out of pursed lips, but the eyes were not so hard and they moistened, so he tempered his reply.

'Tell me where this Briar Cottage is and I will pay her a visit.' He watched those eyes shift a little; she had to answer him, but there was unwillingness there at the same time. Why?

'Well, sir, you could go there yourself or I could send her word.'

'That will not be necessary.'

'Very well. I thought a man of your position, though, would not venture to . . .'

'I shall take the burden of thinking for me from you. Where does she live?' He watched her eyes dry and daggers sharpen within them as she glared back at him. Good, Christian thought; he could not abide tears, but hatred he knew how to deal with.

'Well, if you follow the path from the rear door of the Hall down through the walled garden, then venture out by the east gate passing the dogwoods, you will see that opposite there is a lane that goes into the old woodland. Briar Cottage is a twenty-minute walk along it, set back a ways. You can't miss it as her herb garden is well-tended and that beautiful rose border is divine. Her lavender hedge is something to savour when in full bloom; excellent to use for a bad sleeper, too.' The woman's words actually lifted with some admiration.

'Thank you,' he said, thinking that if he needed a gardener, perhaps the amazing Mrs Jennings would be able to advise him on where to find one of them also — that was, if she wasn't too busy being the cook and housekeeper to help. She appeared to be invaluable.

'She may not wish to return, though.' The statement was stark, but Mrs Hitchins did not embellish it further.

'Why ever should she not? If I make her a more than generous offer, which should be agreeable to her, I am sure she will see the sense of it. No one is going to try and revoke her rights to the cottage. Is there another reason? Was she dismissed from service under a dark cloud? I should know if there is a stain on her character. Please tell me now?' he asked, sensing this woman was deciding whether to risk passing on some titbit of gossip to her temporary master or not.

'She was abruptly dismissed when her mistress died. It was not done in a kindly way, after over fifteen years of service to the family. Mr Howard and his wife were not . . . well, they had her removed along with her things to the cottage on the same day. Mrs Jennings was very hurt by the insensitivity of her dismissal.' She sniffed again.

'Do you have a cold?' He snapped his question out and saw Mrs Hitchins brace herself further.

'Indeed not!'

'Good! You make this claim, yet this Jennings woman was bequeathed a cottage for life — is that not amazing generosity in recognition of her loyal service?' he asked. There was something he was not understanding about this situation.

'Her mistress thought highly of her, and made sure she would have somewhere to go should she be no longer needed to care for her.' Mrs Hitchins did not sniff, but swallowed this time to control her emotions.

'Speak plainly, please. Is she of good character — was there any reason why she should have been 'removed' so quickly?' he persisted.

'Mrs Jennings is a woman second to none. She is kind, gifted and an excellent companion. There is no stain on her character, sir. Mr Howard, however, had not known about the arrangement for her living, and it upset him and his wife. They could not upturn it, although they sought legal advice on the matter, as the dowager owned the cottage and the acreage that it stood on.'

'Good. Well, then, she would seem to be the best person to approach at the moment. Please make enquiries about your replacement. Now, I require you to make a list of the staff we need to get this place running properly again. I would also like to see the household accounts for the last six months, the inventories of what the Hall has in its stores, and a list of repairs that you are aware of that need doing in order of their urgency.' Her eyes bored into him, but he did not change his stern expression as he waited for her comment.

Her lips tightened. 'I was just going for some air, before I started my day . . . again, sir.'

'Well, you can do that later. Today, I need you to provide me with information that was missing when I made the purchase. Now would be a good time to begin it — straight away, in fact! I take it you have breakfasted — if not, feel

free to help yourself to what is left — but I want the task completed today.'
He did not give her the chance to walk away from him again.

Christian stormed out of the doorway. He would not give the woman time to warn this paragon of virtue Mrs Jennings, who resided in her garret beyond the dogwood trees, of his arrival, or of his proposition of a return to his employ. Instead, he would take the air and catch Jennings unaware of his intentions.

He was a good judge of character and did not suffer fools gladly — Howard had been a prize fool, for Christian could plainly see that this estate had great possibilities, and the man had lost it on the turn of a card before losing his wits and finally his life. Christian aimed to make it good and to stay there. He was done with war and losers. His future was just beginning.

★　★　★

Eleanor awoke feeling rested, even though her bed had been little more than one built into a wall cupboard with a narrow cotton-covered mattress roll at its base. Filled with cloth or wool clippings, and just wide enough for her to lie straight in, it had been passably comfortable and snug. Certainly it was a warm cocoon as the cold from the flagstones was such a shock to her. The carpets, wooden floors and warm fires of Kinsley had not prepared her for the cold that permeated this small cottage.

The quilted cover was one that she recognised from her nurse's room in the Hall. A grown man would have never fitted into the bed, but for Eleanor it had been a welcome, safe space in which to lose herself; to forget her troubles and feel warm and cosseted. One thing she could not abide was to shut the doors, feeling trapped inside.

Sitting up, she stretched out in her shift, swung her legs over the side and slipped her boots on as she stood. The

Yorkshire stone-flagged floor generated cold even through the clipped mat. Once her bed roll was neatly stored again, Eleanor took her day dress off the hook inside the door, then found her brush in her bag and closed the bed cupboard back up — how strange it was, she thought, to sleep in a cupboard! Yet it appealed to her childlike curiosity — a secret space, a hidey-hole. Eleanor and Howard had played in a tree house when she was a carefree child. How long ago those days seemed now. She smiled and felt sad, because Howard as a child had been fun and she had enjoyed his company, but once sent away to boarding school he had changed. Pompous Howard returned and grew more remote, turning into a braggart and then a gambler. Next his love of drink took over, dulling his wits when he married Lady Jemima Tuxton. Eleanor blamed her more than the war for her brother's early demise. The woman's ambition knew no boundaries, and now she had even taken off in the Kinsley coach.

Slow snoring emulated from the small four-poster bed, which Eleanor recognised as the old nurse's one from Kinsley Hall. The rhythmic sounds told her that her host had not yet woken, so she carried her things through to the kitchen where the stove gave out some little warmth. It was the quickest she had ever dressed in her life, and unaided; usually a maid set the fire for her before she awoke so she never had to dress in the chill morning air.

Deciding that if this was to be her temporary home she may as well find out where things were, Eleanor peeked into the larder and decided to help herself to the food within. Minnie kept an orderly cupboard. That was reassuring, as she had no wish to find out she had mistaken borax or rat poison for a condiment.

Eleanor removed a large bread bap and found a serrated knife and board so that she could cut a piece, which turned out to be more of a wedge, but it made her smile with satisfaction that she had done it herself.

She ate the buttered bread and honeyed ham, washed down with a small glass of warmed milk. She had found a jug in the cold-store cupboard at the back of the kitchen. How strange this feeling was, though, of not waiting for food to be handed to her; it was one of exploration into another world where she made all the choices amongst the very limited fare, rather than being presented with what the housekeeper had agreed with Jemima should be eaten. It might be a novelty that would wear thin, but at that moment there was something strangely appealing about making things for herself; at least for the time being.

Eleanor opened the shutters of the cottage's living room, letting the light flood inside. Then her eyes focused on the well and she almost burst out of the cottage and ran to the path to where she retrieved the bucket and fetched up a pail of water. Who would have thought that doing these things was so refreshing? Soon she had returned to the warmth of the kitchen range and the kettle had heated her water through, so she washed quickly before dipping her brush into a bowl of water. Eleanor bent over double, running it through her long, dark chestnut hair with careful and slow strokes so as not to cotter or put new tangles in it. She smiled, enjoying the feel and sense of freedom as it flew freely behind her back when she flicked it loose over her shoulders. The colour contrasted beautifully against the lemon floral print of her day dress.

When a sharp knock broke her moment of peace she was surprised. Without thinking she almost skipped along the passageway to open the cottage's sturdy front door, deciding it must be Samuel returning with some dairy from the farm as he knew she was there. But instead she was faced with a tall gentleman who, looking as surprised to be greeted by her as she was to see him, removed his hat to reveal a head of thick, shoulder-length, raven hair. He hesitated before speaking then said two very simple words, showing his obvious disbelief as he uttered them.

'Mrs Jennings?' he asked, incredulously.

'Yes, I mean, no . . . I am not she, but this is her abode.' Eleanor was suddenly aware that her hair was loose, cascading over her shoulders, and that it was not even properly dry. She, an unchaperoned lady, was standing before this gentleman in a humble cottage dressed in a fine day dress. How strange her situation was! It made her feel quite vulnerable.

'Who should I say is calling, sir?' she asked, and saw a smile appear on his face.

'Who is calling?' he repeated, apparently lost in thought; or maybe, she wondered, he was a little simple.

'Perhaps you could leave your card, sir . . . ' she said, and saw a glint of humour in his eyes as he laughed at her.

Of course he would not expect to leave a calling card here . . .

'Is Mrs Jennings in?' He leaned more on one leg than the other, holding his hat casually in his fingers. She did not care for his tone. It was as if he had had enough of bothering with her nonsense and was dismissing her.

'Who is it who would like to know?' Eleanor could be equally direct, she thought.

'You are?' he queried, ignoring her request and laughing again when she folded her arms in defiance. The man was arrogance personified, she thought.

'Ellie?' Mrs Jennings bustled up the corridor quickly behind her. She must have heard the knocking and thrown on her dress and wrapped a shawl around her shoulders quickly, hiding her hair under a bonnet.

Before Ellie could answer, she was pulled back and the formidable form of Mrs Jennings blocked the doorway. 'I am Mrs Jennings, sir, so what business is it you have with me?'

Eleanor took a step back, but watched this handsome and overconfident man address her protector directly.

'I am Sir Leigh-Bolton of Kinsley Hall. I am the new owner, and I have it on good authority that you are a gifted cook and housekeeper, so I would therefore like to speak to you about a position, if you are at all interested. I would rather not do this on the doorstep, but I am in need of both positions to be filled with immediate effect, and have heard that you are more than able to do either . . . Although a cook would be my top priority,' he said, and smiled charmingly at her. He raised his head slightly as Eleanor reacted to the shock on seeing the man who had somehow taken her home from her brother, and gasped.

'Well then, you had best come in. This is all a bit unexpected. You need to give me a few moments to collect meself and then we'll talk proper like.' She turned around and winked at

Eleanor. 'Now, lass, go set yourself to task in the kitchen and we'll sort something out for the gentleman to eat . . . ' She all but pushed Eleanor along the corridor before turning and insisting that Christian sit in her small parlour a while whilst they gathered their wits.

'We'll not be long. You can read the Good Book or admire the view of me garden — not that it is as grand as yours — and then we can have a chat, sir . . . as in . . . a 'Sir', you say?' she asked, just to clarify things.

'Yes, as in a 'Sir',' he said, and seated himself awkwardly on a chair.

'Well then, I best get me best china out!' she said, and laughed.

Eleanor was re-boiling the kettle, but she stood with arms folded to face Minnie as she entered the kitchen.

'That man has stolen my home! Minnie, you let him come in here!' She fumed and dropped her fisted hands to her side, turning away and staring at the small range as if the heat of her temper would make the water boil more quickly.

'Calm yourself, lass. This could well work to your favour.' Minnie sat Eleanor down on a stool and handed her a brush. 'Make yourself respectable and come back in here. Don't you go fronting him, 'cause Minnie has an idea that will get you back in your home and to a place where you can sort out them things you never got a chance to do — but girl, you have to be quiet and humble. Dull the fire in your eyes and the spark-firing words from your tongue. We can help you, but not if you go showing that temper!'

'How?'

'Do as I say, lass, and follow my lead. His type won't stay around a place like Kinsley long; he'll miss his clubs, and that will work to your advantage. Now run along.'

Eleanor did as she was bid, but her heart wanted to go into the small front room and tell the man who stole her home what a vulgar rat he was. But this was Minnie's home, and she would respect the woman's advice — for now.

5

'Well, now.' Minnie swung her front room door and propped it open with her body whilst she let Eleanor pass her.

Eleanor carefully brought the tray in sideways so as not to knock the edge and risk spilling the tea on the white embroidered tray cloth that covered the old wooden stained surface nicely. She could not help notice it had the monogram of her mother's initials on it; but seeing as Minnie had been her close friend and companion, she could hardly hold a grudge against the woman making use of it. She knew that 'Sir' was watching her keenly. Whatever Minnie's plan, they had not got off to the best of starts; she tried so hard not to glare at him.

'Place the tray down on me table, Ellie.' Minnie smiled and straightened her posture genteelly as she oversaw its safe deliverance.

Eleanor's hair was neatly pinned up and she looked more like her normal well-presented self. Sir moved his booted leg so that she could place the tray carefully and squarely down on the small table.

'Lovely, I'll pour. Come, Ellie, and sit on the window seat whilst Sir . . . '

'Sir Leigh-Bolton is my title, Mrs Jennings,' Christian repeated, but his eyes were fixed upon Eleanor rather than Minnie.

Eleanor tried not to laugh at what had been referred to as the window seat, as it was no more than a plank of wood atop a stone sill.

'Well, Sir Leigh . . . '

'Sir will do, thank you,' he said.

'Aye, well, sir, you want me to go back to the Hall as a housekeeper or a cook, is that correct?' She folded her arms under her bosom after she had carefully poured out their drinks.

'As a cook would be preferable, but if

you are concerned about the financial reward, as my situation is desperate, I am content to be generous.' He smiled; his eyes were now meeting Minnie's stare.

'Very well, but I am only one person and, although very adept, you need two.' Her words, as always astute and forthright, surprised Eleanor as she was speaking to a gentleman so directly; but then Minnie had her own cottage, it was her home that she loved dearly, and it was he who needed her skills. How quickly the tables turned in this new world that Eleanor was having revealed to her.

'Yes, that is very true. You understand the situation well enough. Mrs Hitchins has sought a position elsewhere, so I am slightly bereft of staff and local knowledge at the moment. I was hoping you might know where the Hall's previous staff fled to.' He tilted his head slightly and looked to Eleanor, who was following the conversation keenly. Yet, she managed to withhold comment until the last statement had been made.

'They did not flee; they were dismissed without warning when the Hall was . . .'

'Yes, Ellie, I am sure that Sir is concerned with resolving his own problem now, rather than dealing with the torrent that flowed under the bridge when Mr Howard left the place to him.' Minnie cast Eleanor a warning glance.

He raised his hand in a gesture to silence Minnie, which Eleanor found quite amusing. As Minnie's eyes glared at the side of his head, he addressed Eleanor directly.

'So, you say that the last owner left his Hall and staff to fend for themselves? I understood he had a wife, a son and a full complement of staff here. The wife and son were to travel to relatives in Kent, but the Hall and staff would be kept on until I arrived and took over.' He looked from one to the other.

'Was that all you knew of the people who lived in the Hall — no mention of any other?' Minnie asked, as casually as she could do without raising a query from him.

Eleanor was astounded that she had not been mentioned amongst the list of goods and chattels, even. She saw Minnie's frantic, silent warnings to bite her tongue and decided to do just that.

'That is what I understood, miss. Was there more?' he asked. His eyebrows rose.

'Well, you'll be missing a coach, as it went with the wife and son to Kent.' Minnie sniffed, changing the direction of the conversation quickly.

'Well, that will be returned in time, or compensated.'

If Minnie worked in the Hall, then Eleanor might very well be able to gain complete access — and that would mean that her things, those that were rightly hers, could be regained discreetly.

'I have no idea how the Hall was sold on to a stranger, sir, that was not my business, but there were many people who had to suddenly find employment elsewhere, and these are hard times. Many of the local manor houses have a full complement of staff already.' Minnie took his attention back to the matter in hand. 'The poor men who returned from war are suffering still.'

'Yes, as someone who has served my time, I am well aware of the plight of many of my men who came back slightly broken, only to be further dispirited.' He cleared his throat as if he had strayed from his intended course slightly. 'Well, then, if you two could help spread the word that we are restaffing, I will interview and re-employ anyone whom I see fit to do an honest day's work.'

'We will do just that, sir, but if I may suggest one immediate solution: you could do a lot worse than take on Eleanor as your housekeeper, at least for the time being. She knows the Hall well, and I would be happy to do some cooking for you as long as I can live in me cottage undisturbed — you do know that I'm entitled, don't you?' she added.

'Yes, I do, but that is not why I am here. I have no intention of trying to take your home from you!'

'You'd have a job trying,' Minnie said, in a moment where her guard and sense slipped.

'Mrs Jennings, I have laid siege to enemy villages, villas and towns. Believe me, if I wanted you gone it would be easy to achieve. The well could have an unfortunate accident, a spillage of some detritus with no witness to testify, then where would you get your water from? The river rights are mine. The paths you must tread to leave your cottage are all on estate land. The goods you barter are grown here, but I could stop my workers trading my goods. You see how an evil landowner could make you leave without venturing to court? But, please be assured, I am not an evil man. Only occasionally would I ask you to stay at the Hall, or in bad weather when leaving it would be ill advised.'

Eleanor stilled. These words were not meant as threats — or were they? If he was not evil, he obviously knew how to be so.

'Do not look so aghast, ladies. I have no wish to do any of these things, but please let us understand each other; this should be a mutually beneficial agreement.'

Eleanor stared at Minnie in disbelief.

'I see you are a plain-talking gentleman. Very well, I can also be direct. As you say, I have rights, but they are still under your goodwill, so let us not cross words further. I will help you re-staff the Hall, and you take this young lady on as your housekeeper.'

'I . . .'

'Now, Ellie, there is no need to pour out further gratitude. I am sure that Sir realises you and I are doing him a favour when here we are settled with you like my own daughter. Of course, you know the Hall well, having lived there with me for so many years.' Minnie cut across a stunned Eleanor

70

and directed her further comments to Sir, driving a hard bargain; but as Eleanor followed their discussion with no hope of intervening, it became apparent that her earning power had just increased from zero to a moderately generous wage. A good third more than Mrs Hitchins had been given by Howard and Jemima, and so Eleanor smiled.

She would have the keys to the whole house and be invisible. Not seen or heard unless summoned, and she would be able to secrete her belongings away in the cottage over a few months, and then . . . what? Go and stay with her friend in Bath? But then a dark shadow cast over her mind; she had no more friends nearby, she had been set aside by them. Although Bath was a long way from the North Riding of Yorkshire, so perhaps word had not travelled so far of her family's misfortune in losing their home. If that was the case she would gather her things, earn her fair wage, and write to them to ask if she could visit and if they would help her situation. Surely Lord and Lady Blockwood would be kindly in their view; after all, she and Heather had been friends since they had met in Harrogate two summers since. Her uncle was a bishop, so their Christian kindness should surely lift her up again in society. She would still be living at the Hall, wouldn't she?

'Does something displease you about the arrangement, Ellie?' Sir Leigh-Bolton asked.

'Heavens, no! How could it? The lass is speechless. Mind she will have to be called Mrs . . . can't have a housekeeper called 'Ellie', can we? I mean, you don't want to damage reputations. Yours or hers.'

'Mrs what?' he asked, smiling at her. He obviously was not concerned about damaging his own reputation.

Eleanor looked at Minnie, who had faltered. 'Mrs Eleanor Avery.' She smiled, for that was her grandmother's maiden name, and her mother had always loved the woman dearly. Lady Eleanor Gloria Avery was Eleanor's namesake. It was a family name, passed down, but not one he would ever trace as it was on the maternal line. So she told a lie and set her course, one that would become unravelled as soon as a member of her previous staff referred to her as Miss Eleanor with their customary polite regard — unless her presence there as a housekeeper could be explained by Minnie's clever words. It could actually work, couldn't it? The servants had always liked her, the ones that had known her from being a child, so why would anyone deliberately reveal her secret? Visitors might be a problem, but then Mrs Hitchins was always invisible on such occasions, so why could she not be? Besides, it would only be for a few months, and winter meant fewer visitors anyway. No, this could work very well. If not, then at worst she would be thrown out, and she would arrive in Bath earlier and besmirch the man's boorish reputation!

But for now she would not embarrass Minnie, and so played along with the charade.

'Well, Mrs Avery, you had better acquaint yourself with Mrs Hitchins and she can show you the ropes.'

'Oh, it was I who trained Mrs Hitchins, sir,' Minnie said confidently. 'I'll make sure that the transition goes smoothly. And don't you worry none, we'll be there when needed.' Minnie smiled, but as Sir Leigh-Bolton spoke her smile faltered.

'Oh, Mrs Avery will live there for certain. A housekeeper needs to be in her house at all times. I will make sure that a room is made ready, and you will be made comfortable. However, I insist upon this. I cannot have my house-keeper running with muddy skirts back and forth from an estate cottage.'

Minnie's tongue was firmly in her cheek and her ruddy cheeks almost glowed. She had no argument to make against this because there was none to be had.

'Very well, sir,' Eleanor chipped in. 'I presume a room will be made available for Mrs Jennings, so on nights when the weather is foul, as you say, or you have guests and the eating is late, she will have a place to sleep near my own.'

It was Minnie's turn to look surprised.

'Of course, and that will not affect the entitlement to your delightful cottage, Mrs Jennings,' he said politely as he replaced his hat.

Minnie nodded. 'Thank you,' she said, but before she stood up Eleanor had already opened the door to see him out.

He stepped over the threshold before turning and looking down into Eleanor's blue-green eyes.

'Have we met before, Ellie?' he said in a soft voice. Whatever thoughts had crossed his mind puzzled him. 'There is something familiar about you that I cannot quite place.'

'I do not think so, sir,' she answered honestly, for with his fine features, his strength of character that shone through those deep brown pools disclosing hidden depths, she knew she would remember him well enough. Those eyes would have been etched on her memory, of that she had no doubt.

'Strange.' He shrugged, as if it had been a moment's fanciful notion. 'Very well, Mrs Avery, come to the Hall tomorrow at noon and I will take you into York where you can be fitted for your uniform.'

'Yes, sir,' she said as she watched him walk away. When she closed the door she was greeted by Minnie's watchful gaze.

Ellie shrugged at her as if there was nothing to be done about it. Minnie shook her head. 'You should not be travelling alone with a single man with no connection to you.'

'Perhaps not, but would Mrs Avery be fine to travel alone with Sir for the sake of a fitting for new her uniform, Minnie?'

The woman shrugged. 'I need me

breakfast. And you, lass, need to take care. He's a handsome man, not yet thirty I'd guess, but he could also be trouble. We need to think and plan.'

6

Eleanor left her little cosy bed; the sheets were fresh, and out of place in such a humble abode. She smiled because she recognised them from Kinsley Hall. The day was cold, but she cared not, for she was soon going to be stepping back into her beautiful home.

Minnie shook her head at Eleanor as she met her in the kitchen.

'Remember, you are only helping out, and do not let Sir take advantage of you in any way, Miss Eleanor. Just stay quiet, and go about the place as if you are familiar with it, but not like you own it or ever have. Ellie, are you listening to me?' Minnie asked as they walked briskly out of the door heading for the east gate of the walled garden.

'Yes, Mrs Jennings, of course I am. As any housekeeper would to her trusted cook.' Eleanor laughed at the sideways glance she was given.

'This is no joking matter, miss. We have no idea what the man is like, and you are going to have to live a shadow-life keeping your true identity a secret, for we know not what he would do if the truth was known. He did not purchase you with the property, Eleanor. He must never think that. You are in a very vulnerable situation, but if you can keep this position in safety for a few months, you may be able to retrieve enough of your things to send them on to a safe place.' She shrugged. 'Don't ask me where. You have time to think and access your stationery, so you can write to folks, and hopefully someone will come good for you. If not, there is my cottage. The door will always be open, but like he pointed out, I am in no position to speak against him if you sought refuge there without his approval.' Minnie looked far from happy as if she was having second and third thoughts.

'Do not worry, Minnie — sorry, I

should get used to calling you Mrs Jennings again. We shall take each day on its own merit as the good Lord taught us, and see how things unfold.'

She smiled, feeling strangely relieved to be going home. Yet Minnie was quite correct: the man could be a positive ogre, and she would be trapped. But then she thought of his dark features and the glint that had sparked in his eyes when she had unwittingly asked him for his card, and she felt as though he was not a man to fear. After all, Jemima would not be there, so that was something to look forward to.

They arrived at the Hall early enough for them to have a fine breakfast using the Hall's supplies.

'Now, Miss Eleanor . . . ' Minnie began, but Eleanor had let Minnie's jabbering wash over her since leaving the cottage, as she had been lost to her own thoughts and plans. One point she had to discover was how to get her writing box, and the trunk she had stored in the locked-up cupboard in the old nursery, out and into the cottage without being seen. She did not wish to leave either in the Hall. He might have a lady wife! The thought snapped her back to reality. The prospect upset her more than it should have done. They had not even asked if he lived alone.

'That is the problem, Minnie; I never have owned the Hall, or we would not be in the pickle we are in now. You had better get used to calling me Mrs Avery in front of people, and only use 'Ellie' in the cottage. Or our little ruse will be shattered before it has begun. If Sir hears you calling me Miss Eleanor, he may become suspicious.'

'You make a fair point. Perhaps, Mrs Avery,' Minnie chuckled, you could use some of that learning to help me make a full inventory of the kitchen's store-rooms. Looks like they've been kept organised and a deal underused by Mrs Hitchins and the maid, whilst Lady Jemima left with what she could carry. Could be she cleaned them out, but I doubt it. More like let them run down, leaving Mrs Hitchins with little variety to live off.

'Ah, Gertie! Glad to see you again, lass!' Minnie looked up and greeted Mrs Hitchins with a warm hug, smiling at the woman who entered with equal enthusiasm. Obviously the burden of being the only member of staff with any position of authority was too much for her, even when the Hall had been left empty of family. For the next hour they went through the much-depleted stores with military precision.

'Oh, Minerve, how much I have missed your lovely company here. Sir Leigh-Bolton asked me to make a list of the staff and the supplies needed to get the Hall running properly again. I did try, but my heart breaks for the life we had before all of this nightmare unfolded. Can you look over this and let me know if I've missed anything off?' The woman came in and sat down at the table where there was already tea and cake placed ready for her. Mrs Hitchins had not seen Eleanor standing behind her just to the side of the archway so, when she moved, Mrs Hitchins' anxious head spun around and she stood up instantly.

'Sit your body down, Gertie. She won't bite. Besides, we need your help also.' Minnie winked as the woman slunk down into the chair again.

'In what way, Mrs Jennings?' she asked, her back ramrod straight.

'Please relax, Mrs Hitchins, I am no longer here as a daughter of the Hall. Not that that ever did me any good regarding protecting me from being cast out like the staff.' Eleanor heard the bitterness creeping into her own voice and did not like it. She was not naturally a bitter person and had no wish to become one, so she smiled at the nervous face of Mrs Hitchins, politely.

'Well, fortunately for you, lass, you were not cast far, and now fate has brought you back here nice and safe.' Minnie looked at her with more than a little note of rebuke in her voice.

'I am more than grateful for your hospitality, Mrs Jennings. I did not mean to sound as though I was not. Forgive me, please.' She smiled and saw a look of approval cross Mrs Hitchins' face.

'Accepted! Here, set yourself on that stool and I'll fix your hair, and let's get that ribbon straight on your lovely straw bonnet. Then you can travel into York looking respectable, like a lady should do. No one must suspect that you are any less than you were, if you catch my meaning.' Minnie winked at Mrs Hitchins, but Eleanor really did not understand, other than that she was to return brazenly to the city with Sir Leigh-Bolton to be outfitted as a housekeeper, to serve him in her own home. How strange fate was! What her brother would have thought of it, she had no idea; but then Howard was the one who had left her future in the hands of the selfish woman he married.

Eleanor took her seat as requested whilst Minnie filled in Mrs Hitchins on the details regarding her new employment. With eyes wide and mouth munching a piece of parkin, Mrs Hitchins listened intently as she savoured the warmth of the ginger spice within the cake's bake.

'So you will keep house for him just until a proper housekeeper is found,' Mrs Hitchins said.

'Yes, precisely that,' Eleanor said quickly, deciding that this was a far more plausible explanation than admitting she was planning to live there under subterfuge for the foreseeable future. If word got out to anyone who cared to gossip, it could also be plausible, as she was helping Sir amicably with her own future still in abeyance, with Mrs Jennings as her chaperone like she had been for her mother.

'And then he will find you a suitable position elsewhere? A governess or companion, yes — that would be good, like our Minnie was to your own mother. That worked very well as she has her own cottage now big enough to house a small family.' Mrs Hitchins nodded at Minnie as if it was the perfect solution.

'Yes, something like that would be most suitable, I am sure,' Eleanor said, and looked at Minnie — who raised one eyebrow, knowing Eleanor was making up fairy-tales that Mrs Hitchins could happily accept.

'Well, that's for the future. For now, you have to present yourself in the entrance hall and wait for Sir Leigh-Bolton to greet you. Eleanor, I am glad that you decided to wear your damask pelisse. It is a beautiful blue and sets off your eyes well. You do not want Sir to think you a simple country wench.' Minnie smiled.

'Goodness, how could he, when she was born and bred a lady of this Hall? He is brusque, an ex-army man, but he does not strike me as vulgar; just . . . well-opinionated and rather head-strong. Yet, that pelisse is hardly the garb of a housekeeper, even a temporary one,' Mrs Hitchins said in a dry tone of disapproval — or possibly jealousy. Eleanor was not sure which.

'Precisely, Gertie! We want him to value Eleanor and the way she is going to help him out,' Minnie added quickly. 'Of course she should dress appropriately. Like you said, he is a fine-looking young man who has the responsibility of Kinsley Hall resting on his broad shoulders. He will need someone equal to the task of running his new home.'

Mrs Hitchins and Minnie exchanged a knowing nod, which Eleanor did not quite understand, but felt there was an unspoken meaning behind their words.

'What do I tell him if he asks how even a temporary servant is wearing such a quality garment?' Eleanor glanced at Mrs Hitchins' face, as she was obviously trying hard to follow why he should not know the reason. For all the woman's ability to run a house well enough, she lacked any worldly knowledge, and would not suspect for a moment that Sir Leigh-Bolton did not know the truth of Eleanor's position.

'Miss Eleanor,' Mrs Hitchins said simply, 'you tell the man the truth of it and let his conscience be his guide. You should have been able to go to your Aunt Amelia in York, and were callously turned away. He must have some endearing quality, for has he not re-employed Mrs Jennings and taken you under his wing?' She nodded to strengthen the truth of her words.

'Exactly, Gertie . . .'

'Minerve, please call me Gertrude; you know I hate the abridged version of my name.' She flinched as if the thought of it upset her.

'Very well, Gertrude — as long as you call me 'Minnie'! For I hate the proper one given me by my father, who thought himself better than he was, because he had been blessed with the name Montgomery — and he a simple tanner!' She shook her head.

Eleanor smiled as Mrs Hitchins turned her nose up at the thought of the odours relating to this very messy yet important profession.

'My father was a curate; he was to be a priest but, alas, died of tuberculosis one horrid winter. I became a governess and then housekeeper. We never know what life will throw at us, but we survive as best we can,' Mrs Hitchins admitted, and Eleanor did not know quite how to respond.

'Go, Miss Eleanor, and attend Sir, for you want to show that you are punctual, reliable — and, importantly, polite.' Minnie walked with her to the end of the servants' corridor. 'Remember, though, try not to lie outright, but evade the truth for as long as possible. No use rubbing salt into an erstwhile healing wound; you are here temporarily, for you cannot be here when the Christmas ball is thrown, if that tradition is upheld. Not as his housekeeper, anyway, so you have a few months in hand to impress him and collect your things so that arrangements can be made for you to move safely on. If necessary, that is.'

'Of course it will be necessary — how on earth could I stay?' Eleanor said.

'Well, trust in God, lass, for if there is a way he'll set you on it.'

'Very well, Mrs Jennings, I will do as you bid!' Eleanor hugged the woman to her, making Minnie chuckle at the gesture. 'Thank you for helping me,' she said and, humbled by this moment of gratitude, left quickly, entering the main hallway by the door that she had hardly ever ventured through before, as it simply was not her place to do so.

She burst out of the servants' corridor and made for the morning room, as she would normally do when she was kept waiting for Howard or Jemima to arrive, forgetting completely about waiting discreetly in the hallway as she had been instructed.

She stood looking out of the tall window, watching the sheep grazing in the fields that bordered the drive. Quietly overwhelmed by the beauty and simplicity of this familiar scene, she breathed in deeply and thanked God for this moment, which she thought had been stolen from her forever. This had been her home — in a sense it was still — and yet she was here now by choice and not on sufferance, a burden on her brother and his wife. She waited patiently for the intruder to arrive.

She did not have to wait for long.

'Ah, Mrs Avery, there you are . . . ' He walked in holding his tall hat and cane in one hand as he glanced up; his attention had been on straightening the collar of his riding coat as he walked into the room. When he took in Eleanor's form he stopped in his tracks.

Eleanor faced him, her own gloved fingers casually interlocked in front of her buttoned-up pelisse. The high collar served to hide some of the colour that spread across her cheek-bones when she realised the effect her presence had on him. She was either in the wrong place, or he found her quite appealing. The latter thought pleased her, for the feeling was unexpectedly mutual.

'Yes, sir,' she said in order to break the awkward silence that had formed between them. His eyes appeared to have fixed on the brocade that surrounded the buttoned fastening of her coat below her neckline. The high waist helped to give her a longer, leaner appearance than her actual height. The pelisse hugged her arms from above the elbow to her slender wrists; it was her favourite and she wore it well.

'I am glad you are punctual!' His words were stark. He cleared his throat and turned away from her. 'Should we?' he asked, and gestured that she should walk out of the door and make for the coach.

'Yes, we should,' she said, nodding slightly as she confidently passed by him.

She descended the five steps, breathing in the chill of the air at the entrance, and waited as the driver of a fine coach unfolded the step so that she could climb into the carriage. He was a stocky man, of powerful build, his eyes seeming to take in everything without staring directly at her, but Eleanor had not seen him before. That was a relief to her.

'Bill, did you have any joy in York?' Sir Leigh-Bolton asked as she made herself comfortable in the coach. Then she realised that Mrs Hitchins had not been asked to come with them. She should have as the current housekeeper, and as a chaperone to Eleanor, shouldn't she? But Eleanor was not there as a lady but as a servant. The thought excited her, and numbed her senses in equal measure, for she must not be seen alone in a coach with this man by her aunt in York.

'Some, sir. I shall take up where I left off whilst you and the young lady see to your business.' He smiled, which softened his war-hardened face.

'Very good,' Sir Leigh-Bolton replied.

Eleanor sat inside the coach — which, she had to admit, with its gold velvet cushions, was finer than Kinsley Hall's and its old leather-covered ones.

She looked back at the Hall anxiously as Christian placed his foot on the step of the coach ready to enter.

She leaned forward. 'Are we not waiting for Mrs Hitchins to accompany me . . . us . . . ?' she asked, her calm disposition leaving her by the second. What if anyone should see her alight from Sir Leigh-Bolton's coach with just the two of them inside? Word could spread; her already diminished situation would have the label 'ruined' in front of it. She must keep her face turned down and hope that the carriage stopped outside the shop they visited. She was panicking; she should have heeded Minnie's warning, and asked for Mrs Hitchins to accompany her.

'She does not need a new outfit, miss. She chose to leave her position, if you recall.' He was poised with one foot on the step and one still on the ground.

'Yes, but . . . you and I are not acquainted, and . . .'

'And it is a damned cold day; and, unlike my man Bill, I am not dressed against the elements as I have no intention on riding atop my own damned coach!' He pushed his way in and dropped into the seat before shutting the door firmly and tapping the roof of the coach with his cane. The vehicle moved forward with a sudden lurch, although he had given her the courtesy of sitting facing forward. She glared out of the window.

'So, tell me how you know the Hall so well, and how long you have lived there.' He placed his hat on the seat next to him and balanced his hands atop the cane as the coach bobbed and lurched along.

'I have lived here for quite a while, but . . . ' Eleanor struggled for the right words to say. Minnie said to stay near the truth when lying. 'I have lived in the area all my life . . . '

He laughed at her. She stopped watching the sheep in the field and stared directly at him.

'What do you find so amusing, sir?' she asked.

'You, miss, for I am delighted to learn that you are an atrocious liar!'

7

'You insult me, sir!' The carriage traversed a rut in the road and lurched forward, which broke Eleanor's moment of indignation as one hand flew to hold her hat, the other to steady herself by grabbing the door handle.

He sat as steady as a rock, balancing both hands atop the cane, his booted feet firmly planted on the coach floor at either side of it. The blackthorn cane had a striking silver wolf's head engraved on its handle. Like its owner, it looked strong, and determinedly menacing.

'No, Miss Eleanor, you insult my intelligence. If your clothes were not too grand for you to have served in anyone else's house, your manner and expectations certainly would be.' He shook his head when she parted her lips to deny his accusation.

'Very well. I shall not insult your intelligence, sir, as it was never my intention. It is true I have not always been in need of taking a position. In fact, this is the first one I will have entertained the thought of; but I am content to be your housekeeper and help you in the transition as owner of Kinsley.' She tried hard to remain calm and retain a voice of some authority.

He laughed. 'That is very good of you. I feel so honoured, Miss Eleanor,' he said, hardly able to contain the sarcasm that filled his every gesture.

It was so tempting to reply that he should be. Instead, she pursed her lips together and composed herself. She really did not want to lose the chance to live for at least a while longer in her own home. *Please*, Eleanor thought, *do not let me end up thrown back onto my aunt's merciless scorn*. She could hardly stay on this man's estate, even in Minnie's cottage, if she fell afoul of his temper.

'Is there anything else you would like

to tell me now, Miss Eleanor, before you leave this coach as Mrs Avery, embracing a new beginning and challenge for such a fine young lady as yourself? I wonder how easy you will humble yourself into the position.' He continued to stare at her. 'Will I find myself living with a harridan keeping a strict house and making demands upon how I run my own household?'

Eleanor fought to control her posture: proud and strong; her manner: genteel, not submissive; and her words: polite but undeterred.

'You flatter my ability and desire to control you, anything, or anyone, for that matter. Do you not understand the position I have found myself in? As many other young ladies of good family have, I am in reduced circumstances, not of my own making, where I have to find a suitable position — governess or housekeeper — in order to survive. It makes no difference to me which; I am more than capable of doing either.' She looked outside at the beauty of the wild moors as the horses pulled the carriage up the steep bank. She could hear the driver shouting encouragement at the animals to push them onward. Soon they would be on what had been a road built centuries earlier by Roman soldiers. The majesty of her surroundings was never lost on her as, even in a coach as fine as this one, she felt so small and vulnerable by comparison to the wilderness outside.

'How did you come to find yourself in such a position?' he asked. 'Help me to understand, as you appear to think that it is beyond me.'

Eleanor did not look back at him until he tapped her knee gently with his cane. Her reaction was instantaneous as her head shot round.

'Thank you. It is not polite to address the side of someone's head, or so I was taught by one of my governesses, if I remember my lessons well.' He waited for her reply.

'I was admiring beauty, sir,' she explained.

'So was I, but having now studied your elegant profile, I would like to hear your honeyed words explain how you came to be in this situation.'

Eleanor was taken aback by his statement — honeyed, indeed! — but she was not so easily taken in by a few flattering words. 'I became a burden to my widowed sister-in-law, and, well . . . it was apparently inconvenient for my aunt to take me in, so I really was left little option.' Happy that she had not lied, or even embellished the truth, Eleanor sat back as the carriage levelled at the top of the bank. Why should she not state it? Her situation had not been caused by anything she had done.

He nodded and paused as if contemplating his next words.

'That is true. I give you full credit, Miss Eleanor, for having a stronger character and a clearer head than that sad excuse of a brother of yours.' His face was set, words direct and body still.

Silence grew between them.

'You speak ill of the dead, so easily.' She did not deny his accusation. He clearly knew who she was.

'Yes, because I speak the truth, and you did not deny it either.'

Eleanor was shocked; he had known all, and yet played her for a fool. 'You were aware that my brother was Sir Howard . . . Why did you not say so straight away? How did you know?' Eleanor stared, disbelief and fear threatening to undermine the charade of being the confident woman she had never been.

'You bear a striking family resemblance to him: the colour of your hair, the light green-blue of your eyes, and the undeniable fact that you stepped into that Hall as if it was your own. Did you really think that for a second I would not suspect you were an imposter to the rank?'

She swallowed and tried to control the moisture that threatened to spill from her beautiful eyes and roll down her cheeks.

'Will you still accept my offer to be your housekeeper?' She clasped both hands together and rested them on her lap in order to steady her trembling feelings.

'No,' he said simply.

Her hand shot to her mouth. 'But why? I know the place better than anyone, and even showed Mrs Hitchins the ropes, so to speak,' she said. 'You could do a lot worse, and I promise not to forget my new place.' Humble, she must stay humble.

'Because, Miss Eleanor, I made a promise to your brother when I visited him before he parted this world. It is one that I wondered how I was to honour when I had heard the family had left for the county of Kent, but I had not realised you had been cast off, rather than swept off with my carriage. Perhaps Howard knew his wife better than you may have realised.' He shrugged and shook his head. 'How lovely his lady wife must be. Then you opened the door of Briar Cottage, an

English rose indeed, the very one I was about to seek out.'

'What promise was that?' she asked, her words little more than a whisper. She did not dare voice her thoughts on Jemima lest he think she did not deserve the title of 'Lady' either.

'To find you a suitable husband.' He stared at her as his words sank in.

'Well, you can be relieved of that burden, for I am certain I will find one myself.' She felt the panic rise within; it made her hands shake, hopefully not obviously, as her grip tightened.

'By being my housekeeper, wearing a dour dress and living in the shadows, being called Mrs Avery?' He chuckled. 'You have as much chance of finding a suitable husband like that as Napoleon did of winning his last battle.'

She breathed deeply, cheeks burning as the Minster spires came into view. She must be calm.

'Love finds a way . . . You should have more faith, sir. Howard was obviously delirious, because you did not even know me, and he would not leave my future to a stranger's whim!'

'Love! You think love enters into this equation at all?' He shook his head. 'You need to be looked after, provided for, and I intend to make sure that this happens. Has it occurred to you that on his dying bed he thought me the honourable and trustworthy man that he could never be?'

'You have no authority over me, or my life!' she said, as confidently as she could.

'That is where you are wrong, Miss Eleanor, for I have absolute authority over you. Howard made me your guardian. You are twenty, and I am about to take you to my legal advisors in the city, where papers confirming my ownership of the Hall, and my agreement regarding your guardianship, will be confirmed. You will be advised as to your options, but then you must for your own safety see sense.'

'But . . . but . . . I . . . '

'You will temporarily act as my

housekeeper, but there is no need to dress like one; I cannot abide the dour figure of Mrs Hitchins stalking the Hall like a ghost. You can help me re-engage the staff needed. You will be able to live in your own rooms, assist your loyal servant Mrs Jennings by overseeing the menus for the week ahead, and be hostess at any social gathering that is held. However, you will not make arrangements to leave the Hall without my approval; you will not invite guests to it without my approval; you will have a limit on the amount paid for your wardrobe, but there will be one — an allowance, that is — and you shall be made aware of when I am at the Hall and when I shall be away; and when I require your company to attend functions elsewhere.'

'You are quite mistaken, sir.' Eleanor thought the man's success at the gaming table, taking the estate from an ailing man, had gone to his head. 'If Howard had left any legal entitlements then I should have been told of them by now. Jemima was brought the sad news by Howard's legal representative, and he did not even speak to me. Therefore, I have every right to make up my own mind what happens next!'

Christian placed the cane along the floor of the carriage and folded his arms across his broad chest. 'Lady Jemima has much to answer for, I'm afraid; and believe me, she will. Not only has she stolen a carriage that did not belong to her, but she has denied you the chance to understand your situation. In short, you could have been ruined. Your aunt, should she have offered, could have taken on your guardianship for an allowance. However, I gather you were turned away, so she was unaware of this also. In the absence of her goodwill, the task has fallen to me. I do not intend to relinquish it.'

'But why? What do you gain by keeping me at the Hall?' Eleanor asked.

'Gain? You really have no idea of honour, do you?' He shook his head. 'Haven't I just explained to you that I gave my word to a dying man?'

'One that you stole away an inheritance from!' Her hands balled into fists as she leaned forward, pushing them down into the cushions.

'Silence!' The word was snapped out, causing Eleanor to instantly regret her foolish outburst.

'I . . . '

'You will never accuse me of that again. A fool challenged me and I beat him fairly, with witnesses present. Nothing was done to steal or cheat the man. In fact, I tried to stop him, but he was so adamant that his fortunes were about to change . . . So do not deride me ever again, or I will give you reason to loathe me for real.' His face froze.

'You would threaten me?' Eleanor said calmly, knowing she had spoken out of anger and had no call to accuse Sir Leigh-Bolton of being a cheat. Yet he was a stranger who wielded such power over her future . . .

'No, I am telling you what will happen if you do not desist from besmirching my good character.'

'I was too harsh, I admit that, but you must see that the consequences of that gamble changed the course of my life irrevocably?' She replaced her hands on her lap. A tremble began again, but she could not blubber like a child. What had been done had been done.

'Yes, I see that, as it has mine. Yours was already heading in a very downward direction, though. Now, I could open new and more attractive options for you. We shall arrive shortly. So please listen, for I will only have this discussion once. I won your home fair and square. If your mutton-headed brother had not been so reckless, I would have let the game pass me by, but there were dishonourable men present who would have taken his Hall simply and keenly.'

'So you are telling me you took it from him as a gesture of goodwill. Pray, if you are so saintly in your actions, then why did you not hand it back to him the next day?' Eleanor was angry, and knew she sounded bitter again.

'Yes, I suppose I did. Besides, the only other possession he could offer up — he did so willingly enough.'

'That being?' she asked.

'You, dear Miss Eleanor! He showed those present your miniature portrait. I took his challenge and won the prize.' He watched her shock closely, but sat still.

His words seeped into her unwilling thoughts. She had been as good as auctioned, but Howard had not gained anything from the deal. He had literally thrown his inheritance and his sister away. Jemima and Sigmund had luckily escaped to Kent. But she was trapped in a home that was no longer hers, with a strange man who thought he had a legal claim upon her. How impossible a situation. How was she to break free now?

'Why did he die?' she asked, focussing on her lap, trying to change the conversation whilst she pondered what had happened. How much her life had changed.

'He drank himself into a stupor, contracted pneumonia, and his organs gave out. He pleaded with me to look after you, or make accommodation for you with this aunt, if she would have you.' He shrugged. 'I thought you must be plain, dull or mischievous for your relative to not want you. However, I see that you are becoming in looks, and you seem to have an interesting yet honest character, so I shall honour his request and see you wed.' He looked at her.

'I have said that is not necessary.' Eleanor was adamant.

'And I gave my word, and that I will not break. This conversation has ended.'

'Oh, has it?' Petulance was not becoming, and yet she found his manner triggered an equally strong reaction to his words. How was she to simply accept this man's influence on her life?

The coach drew to an abrupt halt as the two stared at each other defiantly, neither wanting to break the deadlock.

Bill opened the carriage door. 'Sir, miss.' He lowered the step and stood back. Christian stepped out, collected his hat and placed it upon his raven hair, and picked up his cane. His hand was proffered for Eleanor to take. She did not want to. She wanted to open the other door and run off into the narrow alleyways to lose herself and find solitude somewhere like the Minster where she could pray for help — guidance as to what to do — but she dared not. Reluctantly, she held his hand just long enough to alight from the carriage without losing her balance.

The man, Bill, was looking from one to the other. Whoever he was, he certainly watched his master's back well; that was obvious as he weighed her up and still surveyed the people passing by. To her amazement he winked at her when Sir Leigh-Bolton was not looking.

They entered a building that was old, black and whitewashed walls making its timbered frame look stark. Inside, the smell of lamps and candles mingled with that of old papers, ink, leather and vellum. With the heavy scent of the musk that filled the air from the male clerks that worked at high desks in a room to her left, the place was somewhat airless.

She was escorted into a small office by Christian. Unable to turn away and walk out, she dutifully followed his lead. A man with a monocle balanced precariously was careful to allow her to walk in front of him and into the room where she took a seat. Bill waited outside with the carriage and horses.

'Please be seated, sir,' the man said, and both sat opposite his paper-covered desk. It was busy, not disorderly.

'Now, Sir Leigh-Bolton, I am glad that you have actually located Miss Eleanor.' The man stared at her with a stern and disapproving look.

'I did not have to search far, Mr Copeland; she was in the care of her mother's faithful companion, being looked after on the estate. I am amazed that your man did not manage to seek her out and inform her of the arrangements that have been made. He seems to have only dealt with the lady of the hall, ignoring Miss Eleanor's concern and interest in the situation.'

'Mr Howard's good lady gave her word that she would break the sad news to her sister-in-law in a gentler way.'

'This lady was believed, rather than the man staying and doing his legal duty. She then left with my carriage and two fine horses,' Christian added to stress his point.

'Well, when we were advised that she had left the Hall by a note sent to us by Lady Jemima, and then her aunt had no knowledge of her whereabouts, we became most concerned for her.'

'Was that when you told her aunt that a provision for her care had been offered in exchange for the inconvenience?' Sarcasm dripped from Christian's tongue, but the man shuffled papers and then stared defiantly back at Christian. He was not used to having his professionalism challenged; that was clear even to Eleanor.

Mr Copeland coloured deeply, but his gaze did not flicker.

'I will not live with my aunt,' Eleanor said, breaking the silence.

Mr Copeland glared at her. 'My dear, think of what you are saying. You have left yourself in a precarious position. If you have been seen alighting from that coach with Sir Leigh-Bolton, albeit a stranger to you, your reputation has already been damaged, even if we can find a plausible explanation for where you have been whilst coming to terms with your grief. Do you mean to allow this man to find you a husband as your guardian?'

His words were stark, showing more a wish to go against Sir's wishes than be genuinely concerned for Eleanor. Her aunt also used this legal practice; she knew that from when her uncle, her lovely fun-loving uncle, had died a year since.

'I am stating that I shall not live with my aunt. She turned me away when I visited her before your representative called upon her; she denies this as she denies me too.' Eleanor swallowed.

'I presume you are speaking from your emotional state and not from a logical mind. Women are fickle creatures. Very well . . . ' He addressed Christian. 'Sir, are you prepared to find a suitable match for this young woman? Her reputation may already be slightly besmirched; besides which, she does not have a dowry of note, and has been cast off by her family.'

Eleanor shook her head. Offended, with no point in trying to argue her case, she was going to stand and walk out. Life with Minnie would be preferable to this.

Christian placed his hand on her arm and stopped her.

'Yes, I already have someone of note in mind,' Christian said.

116

Eleanor stiffened.

'Very well; here are the papers. You can sign here and the account will be settled.'

'Can I read the papers?' Eleanor asked.

'No, that would be most irregular . . . ' Mr Copeland protested.

'Let her, then there can be no doubt in Miss Eleanor's mind that all is as we have said.'

Eleanor read, and did not understand some of the legal terms, but was loath to ask the men for further clarification. Yet those that she did understand made it clear that Kinsley Hall was now the estate of Sir Leigh-Bolton in its entirety. *Revoking all other claims to the properties upon it* . . . She pointed to this clause, and asked, 'Briar Cottage?'

Mr Copeland jumped in. 'It has a bequest which will be honoured, but other tenant agreements can and should be updated or withdrawn. No family member can make claim as the estate was — '

117

'Won fair and square . . . ' Christian chipped in.

' — legally claimed by Sir Leigh-Bolton with your brother's agreement.'

'Enough!' Christian took hold of the pen and signed the forms. 'Let it be known that I am now Miss Eleanor's legal guardian, and that should squash all gossip when we are seen together about town. Come, Eleanor, we shall see your outfitter and then take lunch.' Christian stood up and walked out.

Eleanor did likewise, her legs struggling to move for a moment as the enormity of what had just happened hit her hard. Mr Copeland shrugged. 'You best do his bidding, Miss Eleanor; you just gave him absolute power over you instead of returning humbly to your poor, confused aunt.'

Eleanor dug deep to find her strength. She boldly walked out to find the carriage gone and Sir Leigh-Bolton waiting for her. It was hard to judge his expression, but it seemed to be one that was happy with the day's events.

So who had he in mind as a suitor for her? Had he really just won her along with the estate?

8

Eleanor walked in silence. Sir Leigh-
Bolton showed her to a dressmaker's
shop. A bell rang as they entered, which
snapped Eleanor out of her daze. A lady
in a finely made navy dress approached;
the white lace that edged her garment
was stark, but immaculately made and
starched.

'Can I be of assistance?' she asked
— eyeing Sir Christian appreciatively,
Eleanor thought.

'Yes, my ward needs three complete
new outfits: a fine silk for dinner
parties, a warm walking dress and
pelisse, hats and boots, and a complete
set of riding attire.'

Eleanor stood there watching the
colour rise in the shopkeeper's face as
she no doubt calculated the profit to be
made.

'If you fulfil this order to my

satisfaction, then we shall open an account.'

The woman smiled and nodded back at him. 'Of course, our work is second to none. Leave your ward with us and we shall take all the needed measurements.' She looked at Eleanor. 'If you would come through, miss, we shall begin.'

'Good,' Sir Christian said. 'You may add on any bits and pieces as needed; but not to excess, Eleanor. I shall return in an hour.'

'Thank you,' she muttered, and walked through to the back of the shop, hearing the bell announce his departure. This was not her usual outfitter, but one that had been considered too fancy for Eleanor by her brother and Jemima, although she suspected that her sister-in-law had frequented it often.

It was after a very busy and enjoyable hour that Christian returned to her. She had been given sweet delicacies and the finest tea whilst choosing fabrics and accessories. She reasoned that this was part of her estate that the man had claimed, so why should she not make the most of the opportunity? But, of course, not to excess!

They left the shop and he cupped her elbow. She felt a rush of blood to her cheeks, as this was indeed a forward gesture. Or would it be considered so for a guardian? Yet certainly not one acceptable from a stranger.

They stopped outside an old coaching inn now boasting its services as a fine hotel with new extensions to the rear. Here, travellers could stop and take refreshments between coach rides if continuing on to a further destination, or stay and enjoy the ancient city that was developing with grand stone terraces. It had a fine racing track but, unlike Harrogate, lacked a spa.

Eleanor waited with her guardian to be seated in the recently opened dining room. The idea seemed absurd even to her, for she did not know this gentleman. Yet here she was in a city where she was known by some of Sir Howard's society friends, with her escort, who was as unknown to them as he was to her. How strange fate was. She glanced around at the surprisingly light dining room, which had been recently decorated to have a pale cream plaster between the heavier, older, darkened wood beams. She fought to keep a calm composure, reasoning that even if Sir had been some distant cousin who had arrived to claim the estate, he would ultimately have been just as much a stranger to her. She ignored the little voice of conscience that niggled at her, telling her this present situation would be her ruin, for at least then he would have been her relation and not just some strange man who had won her home from a drunken buffoon. His pleasant fashionable appearance made it feel all the more wrong to her. If he were ten years older or so, perhaps he could have passed off as a distant uncle figure. But he was splendidly handsome and in his prime.

Eleanor forced a relaxed expression onto her face, an ironically difficult thing to do, as she recognised a few people from her brother's social set. Sir Thomas Ellerby was one such; she nodded acknowledgement across the room. He was seated with his wife but the indignation on the man's face was clear. Their eyes were taking in every detail of Christian's fine bearing and apparel. Whispers were exchanged; their presence had been noted. This was obviously a fashionable place to eat as well as a convenient one for travellers. Eleanor had never been before. Heads turned as they were escorted to a table, but Eleanor smiled confidently back as Christian pulled out a chair at a table in the centre of the dining room.

Once Christian seated himself opposite her, he ordered food for them both. His attention then returned to Eleanor, who was admiring the fine stitching on the napkin, wondering where to look next and trying hard not to colour and show how ill-at-ease she felt.

'Eleanor,' he said, in a voice that would not carry, 'this is a fine place to eat. I hope you enjoy the experience, as my man informs me that only the best of people dine here.' He smiled, obviously finding humour in some private joke he had with his man Bill. For a master and servant, they were uncommonly close, Eleanor realised.

'Are you making a point, sir, or simply trying to embarrass me?' She sat upright, a strange feeling of daring and rebellion giving her false confidence. Eleanor just hoped it would hold. She had no wish to end up running out of a place like this in public shame.

'Which do you think?' he asked. He gestured for the waiter to come and serve them their wine.

'You are like a lion staking a claim in some way . . . You are making a point, announcing your arrival to the city and that I am a part of the estate you have inheri- . . . won,' she said, and waited as the waiter returned with Christian's choice of wine. He carefully poured hers into a crystal glass, and she was surprised at its fine taste.

'Excellent, thank you,' she said, and the waiter took his leave.

'Exactly!' Christian said. He also tasted, and obviously approved of, the wine before drinking a hearty mouthful. He acknowledged an acquaintance across the dining room.

'I am the lawful, rightful owner of Kinsley Hall, and you are not to view yourself as part of my 'winnings', dear Miss Eleanor. You are from this day forth, and by your own agreement to it, my ward, and rest therefore under my protection. We have nothing to hide from these people, and they are the swiftest way I could think of to spread our good fortune throughout the region; so let the gossips do their worst if they see fit to. We shall remain above it, and shall enjoy our liberty.'

He was smiling with such ease that Eleanor realised he meant every word. This was not a charade to him. She concluded that the meeting in the legal offices had taken a weight off his shoulders; he looked far less troubled, and a few years younger as a result.

'You said that you had someone in mind for me, sir, a suitor; but you must accept that I do not wish . . . '

'Eleanor, that is for the future. Just enjoy the present. I want to know all about Kinsley, so do tell. You are a wealth of information on the subject because you were part of its past, and shall now help to forge its future. So, tell me, who is the . . . ?'

'You have the gall to dine in here amongst civilised folks!' Sir Thomas Ellerby had stormed over to their table.

Eleanor replaced her wine glass lest her hand tremble and spill it, glancing at the surprised faces at the tables around them, now all staring at them both.

'Sir Ellerby, won't you and your good lady wife join us for dinner? Perhaps we could talk in a more commodious manner if you were seated at my table,' Christian offered.

'You bloody opportunist! You stole away a man's home, his legacy and his life!' His face filled with fury. 'And now you shame his sister with your presence!'

'Come now, Sir Ellerby. Curb your language, please; there are ladies present, and I think you are the one being shamed by your own ill-advised tongue.' Christian dismissed his words with a wave of his hand, yet he was aware that Sir Ellerby was on the verge of calling him out.

Eleanor swallowed. She did not want to look down in shame, as she had done nothing wrong; nor across at the challenging faces delighting in the scene; or at Sir Thomas Ellerby, a man she had hosted in her home at many of Howard and Jemima's dinners. So, instead, she stared imploringly at Christian, who seemed calm beyond measure. Could they leave now without looking cowed or disgraced? she wondered. Would he? Eleanor thought Christian's judgement of what actions of theirs were prudent to have fallen short on this occasion.

'I will not sit at a table with a thief!' Sir Thomas Ellerby blustered, and a wave of gasps escaped from the diners immediately around them.

Christian stood up and looked down at the man, for he was a head and shoulder above him. 'You are misinformed, for your gambling friend, Sir Howard, was drinking himself into an early grave and betting recklessly. I saved Kinsley Hall from a far worse fate, and have secured its future and this young lady's, who I am now grateful to act as guardian for. So you, sir, accuse an innocent man! Now, please either return to your table and your wife, or join us; but do sit down, Sir Thomas.' His words were loud enough to carry.

'Innocent, in whose eyes?' Thomas demanded, both fists clenched by his side. His face looked fit to burst with indignation and yet Christian was not ruffled at all. His even composure helped Eleanor to keep her own.

'In the eyes of the law, sir, as it happens,' Christian said, and raised a defiant gaze. 'Would you see fit to challenge me in the courts if your feelings run so high on the matter? If so, I can give you the details of my solicitor now!'

Eleanor saw Sir Thomas' knuckles whiten, and she honestly believed that he was going to call Christian out; but one man was used to a life of leisure and sport at the tracks and gaming tables, whilst the other was recently returned from commanding men at war. There would be no even challenge for him to face.

'You, sir . . . ' Thomas spluttered.

'Are hungry, and here is our pheasant; so please, join us or leave. You are embarrassing your good lady wife,' Christian said, and sat back down, his attention returning to their food that had been placed by an anxious waiter on the centre of the table.

Sir Thomas stormed back to his table

and threw some money down upon it before ordering his wife to leave with him. Eleanor felt sorry for her: the lady did not know where to look, her face cast down she scurried to the door following her husband, leaving a dinner half-eaten. Sir Thomas passed by their table and meant to topple the wine bottle with his cane so it would spill on Christian's lap, but Christian's reflexes were too quick for him and he caught it before it had hardly moved. The infuriated man blustered out.

Christian smoothly refilled Eleanor's glass before serving food onto her plate. Eleanor was staring in amazement at how composed Christian was throughout the whole scene. The people around them soon lost interest and began chatting to each other again, seemingly not about them. The moment had passed. However, as Christian began eating, Eleanor had not realised she had frozen in time like a statue.

'Ellie, Ellie!' The quiet repetitive tone

of Christian's voice brought her attention back to him. 'Pick up your glass and your fork and start eating, please.'

'Sorry,' she said, and did, and as the motions prompted feelings of hunger and thirst, she realised that time began to move at its normal pace again. People finished their meals and left; some cast cool glances their way, others ones of admiration. Christian smiled amicably back or gave a polite nod of acknowledgement as he sipped his wine. If he cared at all for the derisive looks or the odd caustic comment, he did not show it.

They finished their meal uninterrupted and in relative silence. The food had been like the wine, exquisite. The company had definitely been most entertaining. She had never cared for Sir Thomas Ellerby, finding him loud and coarse, always used to having his own way. His poor wife must have a life of hell, she thought.

★ ★ ★

'Well, Ellie, are you going to admonish me too?' he asked, once they were seated in the carriage again.

Eleanor had been quiet throughout their dinner. He had not pressed her, but left her to her thoughts and to enjoy her food.

'No, I will not. For the law is on your side, even if it appears word has spread that you are no more than an opportunistic rake!' She had not meant to add on the last comment, but he was handsome, he knew it, and some of the looks he attracted from the ladies present in the dining room were flirtatious. One had even dropped her card casually into his lap as she left.

'A rake! Lady, your mouth has done you a disservice. Did I drink to excess? Have I been coarse? Do you know me to be a womaniser who has evil desires upon your virtue?' Christian goaded her, but she could only look upon him as if he were being an annoying sibling, teasing her.

Eleanor shrank back a little into the

soft cushions when he laughed at her.

'What to do with you?' He shook his head.

'Are you any of those things? Were you ever?' she asked.

'No, I am not; and yes, some I have been, but I am no destroyer of innocence. You are safe to sleep in your bed at night without fear of me.' He looked out of the window. 'I will find peace here, and I will not court the favour of those who hypocritically aim to condemn me, for they have had their share of good fortune from your brother's poor skills at the gambling table whilst buoying him up to carry on. Sir Thomas Ellerby is more than guilty of being a party to Howard's downfall, but his ultimate fall was by his own hand, and we all have to be man enough to own our mistakes.'

'So when will you tell me who you have in mind for me as a suitor, sir? Because I will not be forced to marry against my will,' Eleanor declared, and saw his brow crease.

'I had to say something, and I actually do have a notion; but for now, please just let me establish Kinsley Hall as a working manor farm again, and help me to know the people on the estate. You shall not be forced into any match, on that you have my word. But I have told you what I expect of you: you will keep house, you will be a hostess as I am single at the moment, and you will ask me before venturing out. I am happy for you to carry on your life as you would normally, but you will not do anything outside the estate without my permission, for your own safety: on this, there is no exception.'

Eleanor nodded, yet made no promises. 'I have not given you permission to call me Ellie.'

'No, do I need it when we are out of anyone else's earshot?'

'I suppose not,' she said without looking at him, because it had a warm sound to it; or perhaps that was the effect his words had upon her.

'Do you have a fiancée?' she asked.

'Heavens, no!' he said. She had caught him off guard. He had not expected such a bold question. 'Why do you ask?' That humoured glint appeared in his eye.

'You mentioned 'as I am single'. I presumed you intended to marry.'

'Oh, dear Ellie, never presume.' He winked at her, then changed the subject again. 'Very well, Ellie; when we arrive, please tell your accomplices that the truth is known about who you really are, and I will not tolerate any further subterfuge. However, I forgive all this time, as their defence of you is quite touching and shows loyalty that I value.'

'They only wanted to protect me . . .' Eleanor began to defend her friends, but he held up his hand to stop her. So strange to realise she had thought of them as friends and not her servants.

'From what — the opportunist and rake that I am?' he asked, opening his eyes wide, reminding her of a guilty puppy dog professing his innocence.

'From myself, sir, for I was determined to leave, and in so doing discovered I have an aunt who hates me. Why? I have never wronged her. I have always been happy to see her, sing to, or play pianoforte for her. Uncle and I were always so fond of each other. He was always so full of life and laughter. I miss him greatly.' She stopped talking, for emotions began to bubble within for a family that had died out and beloved relatives that had left her.

'Perhaps that is it! You have youth, beauty and talent. You represent things she can never possess again, and you also had captured her husband's heart. These things weigh heavily on a bitter widow's mind.' He shrugged, satisfied with his summation of the problem.

Eleanor did not speak. It seemed strange to her that the woman could have held such thoughts within her, and still smiled and greeted Eleanor when their family visited. How sad she must have been, living a lie.

9

Once out of the carriage, Eleanor went straight to the walled garden. When Christian took himself off on horseback with Bill, she ventured down to Briar Cottage, where she found Minnie, who had finished for the day as dinner was not needed up at the Hall.

Minnie stood up as soon as she saw Eleanor. 'Well, tell me all . . . For as a plan, it seems we fell short of being convincing,' she said, slightly indignantly, as she sat back down in the chair.

'Mrs Hitchins said she would be over shortly, Minnie,' Eleanor informed her as she wondered where to begin.

'Yes, Gertie said as much, so what happened? Did you break down and confess all to him in the coach as soon as those becoming eyes stared longingly into your own? Did he make you tell all, like some cad in a gothic novel?' Minnie asked, her face filled with curiosity mingled with disappointment, or possibly concern that her own situation could be impacted by her part in their naïve plan.

'No! Nothing like that. He knew who I was already. He realised as soon as I opened the door, for Howard and I had features in common. We never thought of that — our eyes. I am not so weak, Minnie. Besides, Howard did think of me in his final days, and suggested that Sir Leigh-Bolton act as my legal guardian. Howard wished it so, and he agreed, so that is that.' Eleanor swallowed, but Minnie's eyes shone brighter than the stars.

'Goodness, lass! You will be the envy of every young maid in the county, for he is such a fine-looking catch. Surely he should know some equally handsome bucks to find you a decent suitor — in time, of course,' Minnie said, and laughed. 'Eee, lass, you have landed on your feet!' She clasped her hands together in joy.

Eleanor did not quite share her enthusiasm. 'Perhaps, Minnie, we shall have to see. I will bide my time before deciding. For I have no wish to have a stranger find me any match at all.'

'Whyever not? You may well be surprised.' The annoying finger wagged at Eleanor and she did not like it.

'He stole my home, Minnie, and so I will take what is mine from it as I planned to and leave, as soon as I am able to have word sent to my good friends in Bath.' Eleanor felt reassured by having a plan, even if it was a very sketchy and unlikely one. It made her feel as though she still had some control over her own destiny.

'Lass, stop and think upon it. This is no simpleton with a title and a fat belly who has arrived at your door, but a fine-looking gentleman with contacts. This is a young, handsome ex-army man who is in his prime. Do you not think he would hunt you down if you ran away? You go against him after he has secured the legal rights to care for you, and you might find you have set yourself in conflict with an enemy who, when treated with some respect, could have been your best friend. Go careful, dear Ellie. Whatever fond memories you have of the younger Mr Howard, cast them aside, for he grew into a man who was not noble and who left you very vulnerable. My advice to you is simple: give Sir Leigh-Bolton a chance to prove himself worthy of the estate, and of you.' Minnie waved an index finger at Eleanor, which was a gesture she was coming to hate.

'I will see, but I will collect my possessions up and store them in my room, in readiness should I choose to leave,' Eleanor said defiantly.

Minnie stood up, hands on her hips. 'Have I ever told you about looking at a gift horse?'

'No, I don't remember you mentioning it,' Eleanor said and smiled.

'Then try!' Minnie snapped her words out as the door opened and a flustered Mrs Hitchins burst in.

'What news, Miss Eleanor?' she asked.

Minnie shook her head at the flustered state of the woman. 'You best sit in me chair. I'll fetch you a tot of something calming. Ellie, explain the situation now, and don't go running on about the future. That is yet to come!'

10

Two months later, Eleanor had been allowed to treat her home as just that. She would rise early, and spend time with Mrs Hitchins and Minnie, arranging the household to bring it back up to a full complement of servants, interviewing staff and sorting out the supplies needed to keep the place functioning. Eleanor was keen to source as much of the produce needed to supply the Hall as possible from the estate.

She had spoken at length with the gardener and Minnie about her plans for the walled garden. She had run her thoughts by Christian first, that they could grow its full complement of produce and have preserves, jams, sauces and dried herbs made for their use, and also to sell on any excess in York or Harrogate markets. This, with the gardener's and Minnie's knowledge, and the added ability of Mrs Hitchins to see how the bottled goods could be made attractive and presented, pleased her. To her delight, Christian seemed enthusiastic about her proposals, encouraging even more of them.

She left the groundsmen and the tenants to Christian to deal with, along with his 'man', who was never far away from his master or the Hall. Even Mrs Hitchins had stopped complaining about him lurking around the place. Bill was the silent figure who solidly served, and yet was never referred to by his surname.

In truth, Eleanor was so busy, and had so many plans that had culminated from years of frustration of never having her ideas listened to before, that she realised when she was smiling at the garden and planning its future the feeling she was enjoying so often now was pure joy. So why should she leave? The answer was simple and stark: she would be married off, and this home could only ever be a transient one. But at least for now it was hers, and so she would enjoy the moments that she could before her future was decided for her. Then she would leave of her own accord.

Christian and Eleanor passed by each other, going about with their different tasks yet sharing the same world. Occasionally they met for a meal, or a drink, and her plans were discussed and accepted with little objection or question. He was quite amicable, and tended to watch her closely, which she took as a sign that he was simply becoming familiar with the notion of being her guardian.

'Eleanor!' Christian's voice shouted through the servants' doorway.

'Yes, sir,' she said as she emerged from the stone corridor into the entrance hall.

'Whatever are you doing down there?' He shook his head; raven hair flipped over his white collar, contrasting perfectly and settling on the finely stitched waistcoat. He raised his eyebrows at her hesitation.

'I was deciding the menus for next week . . . ' Her words drifted off. She had been staring at him, and hoped the pleasant thoughts that had flitted through her mind had not shown upon her face. She found him pleasing to the eye and never tired of watching him — unobserved, of course — whenever she could.

'Well, have Cook come into the morning room, or Mrs Hitchins — you should not be down there. Besides, you have spent enough time with the servants. I want you to regain your position in the house and join me.' He walked into the withdrawing room.

'Join you?' she repeated. 'You want me to visit the tenants with you?'

'Yes, possibly, but let us start by eating together regularly. I wish you to dine with me daily, not occasionally. You shall take your meals when I do, when we are both in.' He was facing her, hands on his hips. The daylight behind him showed his fine figure off. A tall man in breeches and cavalry boots certainly appealed to Eleanor's idea of handsome. It stirred feelings within her that were more than they should be for her guardian. How would she feel if he began courting some fine lady with a dowry and a well-positioned family? The memory of being a burden upon Jemima and Howard resonated in her mind. Eleanor was thinking of Christian more and more as belonging to her in some way.

Eleanor was unsure what to say. She had quite got used to the notion of having her meals with Minnie and Mrs Hitchins, although the latter was due to leave them soon. The thought saddened her.

'Very well. Do you wish me to dress for dinner?' she asked, her mind whirling as she had got used to the informal nature of daily life, and reverting to the formal version did not appeal to her in the slightest; especially if they were to eat making polite conversation or in silence.

He laughed as he watched her standing just inside the doorway. 'No, Eleanor, I do not wish you to dress. I would prefer you to be completely naked. It would make my mealtimes even more entertaining.' He shook his head.

'Your wit surpasses my expectations,' she said quickly, to try and cover her embarrassment, for it was obvious he was being sarcastic and simply making a quip at her expense by using such bold words. Yet the vision of them both being naked together presented a shockingly sinful excitement within her that surprised and delighted her.

'I am so glad that you have some expectations of me, Ellie, for I thought you were hiding from me lest I turn into the 'rake' some would still paint me as.' There was a serious note in his voice.

She approached him as she did not want Mrs Hitchins, or one of the maids, to overhear her short name being used so openly to her.

'It bothers you so much about what people think of you? I thought you were above that, sir, as you dealt with Sir Thomas Ellerby's comments very well, and in a public place.' She looked into his deep brown eyes, wondering what dark and troubled thoughts were making them look less bright than normal.

He lifted a finger and stroked her cheek gently. 'Ellie, please call me Christian. I do not want to hear you call me 'sir' like you are one of the servants.'

'Very well, Christian.' She smiled, liking the sound as the name rolled off her tongue, and the feel of his brief touch as his hand dropped to his side once more.

'I do not give a fig for what people say about my winning this estate. I care, though, that some are tarnishing you with the stain of living with a rake, which is damnably unfair.' He ruffled his hair and stared momentarily at the ceiling.

'It will be my aunt, no doubt, bitter that you have done her out of the allowance she could have had for taking me in,' Eleanor said, and he lowered his chin so they could look into each other's eyes.

'She did that to herself, as she turned you away when you were in need. Shame on her! No, it is more to do with Howard's gambling friends. They are all bad losers, Ellie. They lost their friend who owed them money. I do not owe them so much as a farthing, so they will not get anything from me. If they cannot bring me down, then they will try to hurt a softer target — you. One has even offered to take you off my hands for a small dowry that would clear the debt owed him. I hate the man, I think he has even had the cl- . . . ' He swallowed and shook his head. 'No matter, he will not have you.'

'Who is this man?' she asked.

'No matter; he will not be staking a claim to you, and that is the end of it. But they travel amongst the gaming dens and gentlemen's clubs in York, Northallerton and Harrogate, and spill their poison into the ears of any who will listen.' He shook his head. 'I should have realised that they would stoop so low.'

'Thank you,' Eleanor said. 'I should have said that to you before now, but you must understand that I had lost my home. You care about my reputation and safety, and that is what a guardian should do, so I thank you.'

'Had you lost your home, or had it slipped away before my arrival, Ellie?' He folded his arms casually across his body.

'Well, yes, I am only here by your good grace.' She watched a slow smile spread across his face because she had not fully answered his question.

'You were only here as your brother's burden from the minute your mother left this world. Dear Ellie, your home is more yours now than it has ever been.' He placed a hand tenderly on each shoulder and faced her squarely. 'Admit it. I have allowed you to act as the lady of the house — planning, organising dinners, and even entertaining my guests — without criticism or making further demands.'

Eleanor was not sure what 'further demands' he was thinking about. 'How so?' she asked. 'There have only been three dinners, Christian. I can cope with that.'

He leaned into her, kissing her forehead ever so gently.

She stood there and did not pull away, unsure why he should do such a thing. It was neither threatening, nor did it feel at all paternal. Certainly the sweep of warmth that overcame her senses was not what she had felt on the only occasion her father had kissed her forehead, on her sixteenth birthday. He had not lived long beyond it, sadly.

He looked down at her lips. Before she was even aware, he had moved his right hand and cupped her neck gently whilst his mouth found hers and stole away a kiss.

Eleanor closed her eyes and let the sensation empty her mind of all other thoughts.

He released her and she gasped, taking a small step back.

Their eyes locked, neither turning away,

'Do I offend you?' he asked.

'No, I mean, yes . . . ' She sighed and looked away. 'What is it you want of me, Christian? Do not play games with me, for you are a man of this world who has seen war, and I have only witnessed personal grief at home.'

'Do I scare you?' he asked.

'No . . . but . . . you infuriate me — yes, that is it! You say you want to protect my reputation, and yet you behave so boldly . . . so badly . . . ' She shook her head.

'But, Ellie, do you not see that there is a way that this Hall could be your permanent home?'

'Are you proposing to me?' She could not believe this turn of events. One moment disowned; the next homeless, except for the charity of a servant; then housekeeper, ward; and now . . . this! Her world was moving at such a speed.

'No, of course not, I am asking you to be my mistress!' He snapped his words out in too much of a rush.

Ellie turned to go, but he caught her arm firmly. 'Ellie, my sense of wit is terrible. Of course I mean to marry you! It is just . . . you are beautifully naive, and yet wholesome. I only wanted to tease you as you also infuriate me. You run this house like it always should have been. Forgive me for my clumsy approach.' He released her and smiled reassuringly, or attempted to.

'You are forgiven; but answer me honestly, Christian, do you love me?' She saw the surprise in his face.

Christian stood away looking at her; bemused. 'Did you not feel excitement when we kissed?'

Eleanor laughed. He looked instantly taken aback. How easy it would be to destroy his opinion of himself and his ability to conquer her body, if not her heart. Yet, if she did, it would be all the worse for her and them. Yes, she had felt alive, and wanted to continue. She wanted to hold his neck to pull him toward her, to feel all of him next to her, and yet how shocking these thoughts were.

'You think one stolen kiss would capture my heart? Did you not notice I did not kiss you back, Christian?' she goaded him slightly, not wanting to hurt, but to show him that she was not so easily won over.

'Are you not flattered?' he persisted. She had wrong-footed him, and it made Eleanor feel strangely excited that her words had ruffled his normal calm persona so much. She did not smile, for that would be foolish and petty, but the excitement that filled her was replaced by the feeling of joy because he cared deeply about her, and that meant his love for her was surely growing. He might not recognise it yet, but it was there; and she would embrace it — and

Christian — heartily, but not on the first kiss.

'Yes, of course I am, Christian,' she said softly.

He looked momentarily relieved. 'Then you agree?' he asked.

'I did not say that.' She was going to say more, but they both heard heavy footsteps approaching the doorway.

Both stood apart as if they had not even been talking to each other.

'Excuse me, sir.' Bill's sturdy form appeared in the doorway.

'Not now, Bill.' Christian was most dismissive.

'Please, carry on,' Eleanor said, and began walking to the door. 'We are quite finished for the night.' She walked out without so much as a backwards glance at Christian, who stared after her in disbelief.

11

'I could go away, sir,' Bill said in a light-hearted way as Christian glowered at him, annoyed that Eleanor had taken the opportunity to walk away and leave him without her agreement. The little minx! It might not have been the smoothest proposal ever delivered, but what did she expect? Theirs was an arrangement of convenience on both sides. He was an excellent catch, and she a pretty and useful lady of the house, so why not marry? Then they could have a full relationship and she would come to love him. As for him, he would be happy to have her company and share an intimate relationship with her. What did he know of love?

'Your timing has never been so abysmal, man.' He sighed.

'Really? I thought I normally came to your rescue, sir.' He winked.

'Well, this time I did not need rescuing. I was . . . ' He shook his head. 'I swear I will never understand women.'

Bill came in and stood by a decanter and glasses. 'I don't suppose . . . '

'Help yourself. Pour me one too. So, what is so urgent that you would choose this moment of my greatest downfall to interrupt?' He sat down by the fire and took the offered crystal glass from his friend.

'Is the lady not falling into your carefully-thought-out plan, sir?'

Christian laughed. 'I should have thought it out more carefully. I asked her to marry me, in a manner of speaking.' He swigged back his drink in one gulp, and put the glass down on the small table at the side of his chair.

'She turned you down? She must be mad!' Bill could not hide his incredulity.

'Not really, but she did not give me a straight answer either. How can she prevaricate? I own this estate, her home. I have wealth and am not unattractive. What does the woman expect? I could match her to a fat oaf who wants a young filly to look after him in his dotage, and yet I offer up myself,' he complained.

'Like a lamb to the slaughter,' Bill said, his smile almost breaking into laughter.

'Your point being, man?'

'That perhaps you could humble yourself a little. Appeal to Miss Eleanor's gentler spirit. She may be young. She may be determined to make her home a place that works. But she is still a young lass and they like to feel wanted . . . '

'I want her, that is obvious!' Christian shook his head. He really had expected her to fly into his arms, all her prayers answered by him.

'Yes, sir, but not just in a carnal way.' Bill winked.

'Next you will be quoting the sonnets. Is this really my hardheaded sergeant speaking, or has someone stolen Bill's head?' Christian stared at his friend, knowing that he was the one person in his life who would tell him the God's honest truth in any given situation. He owed the man his life, and that was more than enough to share his home with him for as long as he wanted. Bill had nowhere else to go, so the arrangement suited them both well enough.

'Believe Bill when I tell you that a good woman is worth chasing a little. Do not make her feel that she is simply a convenient option who came with the Hall, sir.'

Christian looked at his friend thoughtfully. 'What does Bill know of such tender things?'

'I was young once, sir. I had me a lovely wife; Catherine, she was. We had three precious summers together. No babbies, which was just as well really, as I would have not been able to look after them, then the war started.' Bill looked down and swirled the golden-coloured liquid around in his glass as if in a trance.

'What happened, Bill?'

160

'She died. The Lord took my beautiful Catherine in a fever that I survived.' He swigged his drink back. 'Life is a bitch at times. So, you like the lass, you take time to make her feel that — wanted, respected. I tell you, one month on she will be longing for you to ask her again.'

'I might change my mind,' Christian said.

'Then you would be a bloody fool, sir, and that you are not.' Bill poured out another.

'So what brings you here? It was not to harangue me on my lack of romantic prowess.'

'Well, we have a game-keeper who should be relocated to the assizes as it seems he has been taking from the tenants, the estate and leading your Mrs Hitchins a right dance — nice woman, that. It's taken a while, but I've sussed out his ways.'

'We shall ride over tomorrow morning and sort him out. You can fill me in on the details over dinner. We'll go to the Hare and Rabbit; I feel like eating out tonight.'

'Very well, sir, I shall tell Mrs Hitchins to inform Mrs Jennings.'

'Mrs Hitchins is still here? She should have left by now, shouldn't she?' Christian had quite forgotten that his housekeeper was supposed to have taken another position.

'Well, sir, you see, it was not really a good idea and she is happy here,' Bill said, and smiled as Christian's eyes looked heavenward.

'Oh well, as long as she is happy. So tell me, then, when was she going to ask me if she could stay and revoke her hastily tendered and accepted resignation?' His tone was very sarcastic as he stared at Bill, who was still smiling at him.

'No need, sir; Miss Eleanor told her it was advisable for her to stay on.'

'Bill, she is a block of ice, I do not need to see her ghostly form drifting around the shadows of my home,' Christian said.

'Ah, you are too harsh by half.

Gertrude is a gentle soul and you scared her. Give her a chance too.'

'Good grief, you and Gertrude are friends! You cannot be serious, you and the ice-maiden?' Christian ran his hand through his hair. 'These women are infuriating to me. Ellie did not jump at the chance of becoming my wife. I told her the Hall could be her home again. I have a good mind to send her to a convent to think it through. Then she might look more kindly upon my offer.' Christian refilled his glass.

'That would be unwise, sir. She has an eye for you, but you need to ingratiate yourself. The lass has had shock on shock, and you come in and take over the place and expect her to be grateful within a few weeks. She is spreading her wings and learning to fly: give her time before you clip them.'

'Fetch the horse, Bill, we will ride into Gorebeck. I think you need some fresh air. I know I do.'

Christian stormed out, whilst Bill downed one more glass for the road.

'Well, what did you find out about Squires?' Christian finally asked Bill once they were established in a corner settle in the Hare and Rabbit.

'It appears he has been threatening the tenants. Scaring them into paying more, in kind if not in rent, with eviction. Claiming to have the new master's ear and warning them against speaking out.'

'Damn the man!' Christian shook his head. He had given the man the rope with which to hang himself. Wanting to know who he could trust and who not, Christian, via Bill, had given people on his estate tasks to do: the responsibility for their part of the working of the estate, to see who came through with good and honest hard work which would show its own reward through their resulting goods or crops, provided they were honest, and would reveal who abused the opportunity and his trust.

Samuel had proved to be a good and

honest man at the dairy farm. Hitchins had been a pain to Christian, dour-natured whenever he was around, but Eleanor had praised her immaculate records and housekeeping abilities. Cook was frugal, but always provided edible fare; the stable hands had spent wisely on improving the stables; the gardeners had only put some aside for the odd nip of brandy to fend off the cold they often worked in; but the man who had proven himself to be a cheat, bully and liar was the groundsman. It had taken Bill a few weeks to gain trust and unearth the truth of what had been going on in the background, whilst the man presented a working estate, subject to sheep rustling and poor crops through lazy tenants. The truth was, he had been selling off small numbers of sheep regularly, and taking part of the farmers' profits to line his own pockets.

'Do you know when he next plans to round some up, and with whom?' Christian asked, keeping his voice low, well below the noise and banter inside the place.

'No, not precisely, but I have been following him these last few days and he was seen with Jason Mannish three times.'

'Bell Cottage tenant?' Christian remembered the man. Built like a house end. His tenancy was not the best kept, and yet he looked like he had enough to fill his fat belly.

'Aye, sir, and he has been emptying his sheep pen again. Just took six of his sheep to market, sold the wool and the meat, so no intention of keeping the animals for their wool. That is how he does it, a few at a time.'

'We'll need to borrow a few of the Yeomanry, Bill. I want him caught, punished and removed. I do not want anyone else pointing fingers in my direction and swearing I am removing innocent men who served the estate for a long time.'

'Then we should visit their captain in the morning, and I'll tip him the wink when the pen is refilled. Meanwhile, you must come up with your own plan of action . . . '

'Crawled out from under your stone, I see, Low-Bolton!' The slightly slurred voice derided his name as he shouted over to Christian across the tap room. Sir Thomas Ellerby had just appeared at the bottom of the wooden stairwell.

'Thomas, whose bed have you just crawled out from? Not your wife's, I presume,' Christian replied in a light-hearted voice, and was pleased that there was a ripple of laughter throughout the room.

'You blackguard, we are not all made of your low morals,' Sir Thomas blustered as he strode over to Christian's table. Bill had his back to the man, who was focused on Christian alone. When Sir Thomas saw Christian's ex-sergeant look up at him, he did not step any closer.

Four other gentlemen descended the stairs, joking, their banter only ceasing once they saw their friend standing staring at Christian. Obviously to him these men had just alighted from a closed game, and by the expression on Sir Thomas Ellerby's face he had not fared well.

'Come, Thomas, he is not worth your breath. Leave him.' Charles Dewsbury swept an arm around Sir Thomas and the man allowed himself to be turned away, professing how Charles had prevented him from calling Christian out, but going willingly enough.

'You know, sir, if I could find some dirt to dish on that bastard I would happily do so,' Bill said watching Sir Thomas' back.

'I know, Bill, but he has friends who have friends, so to make anything stick fast to him, it would have to be good. It would have to go beyond the local magistrate, one Charles Dewsbury, and to an independent authority who could usurp their band of rogues.'

Bill sat back and grinned. 'Hmm, that's what I thought. It would have to be justice which was not meted out by the local magistrate.'

'Bill, stand down, man. I have enough on my plate at the moment. I do not want to have to dig you out of a deep dark cell in York because of a rash act. That man will go the way of Howard. He has debts already.'

'You know this for certain?' Bill asked.

'Yes, for very soon I will call them in.' He looked at Bill and winked.

'Well, I'll drink to that,' he said, and downed the rest of his tankard.

12

Christian and Bill left the inn, and were set on riding back to the estate. The dark of night had engulfed them. Bill was not a man to be taken off guard easily, but when a club hit him from behind as he entered the inn's stables, he fell down like a bull on ice.

Christian waited outside the inn for a few moments, but when all was quiet and no horses emerged led by Bill, his senses were piqued — something was wrong. The natural thing to do would be to go around the to the stable and shout for his friend, but he had been in the army where he had entered enemy villages with his men, watching for snipers lurking in the shadows or on rooftops, ready to ambush them. There was always an unusual stillness to the places when the threat of death lurked. His sixth sense was telling him all was far from well in this sleepy northern market town.

Christian slipped back inside the inn, walking past the serving hatch and beyond the tap room. Only a few heads turned. He stopped in the short corridor before the back door, where he loaded his pistol.

Slipping outside again into the cold night air, he kept his pistol to his side and crossed the cobblestones as deftly as he could, entering the stables with caution. A horse was tethered at the back of the inn, but it was not one of theirs. When the club swung at him he ducked, only catching a momentary glancing blow to his shoulder that stunned his firing arm for a second. Bill stood unsteadily, and their attacker fled, jumping atop his waiting horse. Christian aimed and shot. The man yelped as he disappeared around the corner of the inn and galloped off down the open road that led up to Gorebeck moor, then disappeared into the night.

'You alright, sir?' Bill asked, still not

managing to stand up straight. Blood stained the back of his head and jacket. Christian had been about to mount his horse and follow their attacker when his friend sank heavily to the floor. Instantly, Christian was at his side. Bill had fought in battles and not fallen; how could he be felled so easily in a Yorkshire market town at peace — why? Christian looked up at the approaching figures.

The shot had alerted the innkeeper, who arrived with a couple of his men from the inn.

'What the hell happened here, sir?' he asked.

'Did you see who it was?' Christian asked, as he stood straight.

Blank faces stared back at him, glaring at Bill's figure, not comprehending what had happened, any more than Christian had.

'Damnation! Two of you mount up and seek the coward out. He headed up the moor road. The others, get this man inside quickly and carefully! Have him carried to your best room and summon Doctor Hughes. If he is in his bed, insist that I will see to his inconvenience, but get him here as soon as possible. This man is injured. Treat him well, he fought at Waterloo and is a hero this country owes much to.' Christian snapped out his orders, and then turned his attention to his horse that was saddled in the end stall. He felt a wave of emotion sweep through him which bordered on fear. He had not experienced such danger since they were at war, but then his trusty sergeant had always been there to make a joke, take the edge off the death and drama, and watch his back. Now he felt exposed and filled with a strong desire to lash out at whoever had done this.

'Yes, sir,' the innkeeper said, and turned to the men, repeating Christian's instructions. 'You heard him.' Two men rode out at speed in the direction of the attacker, and the rest carried a mumbling Bill into the inn.

His incomprehensible mutterings gave

solace to Christian's ears. The man was tough; he would be fine.

Christian walked down to his horse; perhaps he could catch them up, but his heart wanted to stay and make sure his friend was alright. He had saved his life, when other men had passed by their fallen commander, leaving him for dead on a field in a foreign country. Bill had scouted, found him, and carried him back to camp. 'Damnation!' he cursed. He owed the man a good retirement, a long life, a chance to be happy again.

He stepped into the stall and aimed his pistol as movement at the back caught his eye, but he lowered it when he realised it was no more than a frightened stable lad hiding in the corner; who, thinking his life might be about to end, curled tightly into a foetal position. Petrified eyes staring back at him.

Like a cornered cat he suddenly sprang up and tried to use an upturned pail to jump up and over the partition and into the next stall in a futile attempt to escape.

Christian caught him with his free hand and slammed his slight frame against the side of the stall, taking the wind from his lungs and pinning him there by the neck with one hand. The other pushed the barrel of the pistol to the lad's side. His body slumped as he slid back down until his feet supported his weight on the floor.

The men in the inn may not have seen who the man was, but Christian realised he had just found a witness; he swore on Bill's life he would protect the lad, but find out who had tried to injure or kill them. Unless the lad refused to talk freely about what happened, then he would throw him into gaol and make sure he did not see the light of day until he spoke.

'Who was it?' Christian shouted at his frightened face, watching him flinch.

The lad tried to shake his head.

Christian released his grip and stood back, but the pistol was trained on the lad; he was going nowhere.

'I will ask once more, and you will tell me the God's honest truth, or you will go down in chains into the lock-up; and, believe me, I will hold the key to your release and no one else,' Christian promised, not shouting but speaking plainly in a normal voice. 'Tell me now!'

The lad shook his head at his words.

Christian realised that for him to refuse meant that whoever had lain in wait for them must have a strong influence, frightening the lad out of his wits and senses, for he was scared stiff and had a gun pointed at him.

'He'll kill me . . . I didn't see nought . . . ' He swallowed and tried to bravely put his chin up. Tears fell from the corner of his eyes.

Christian would have felt pity for him if it was not for the blood that had stained his hand from the back of his sergeant's head.

The lad was just about old enough to be a drummer boy. Cannon fodder. But he would not need to be that anymore.

Bill and Christian and those who had fought for most of their adult lives had seen to that for him. But Christian was in no mood to be lenient to a frightened pup that held the name of a man who had tried to take them down.

'They'll come out of the inn. They'll not let a stranger hurt me,' the lad said as he sniffled.

Christian realised he had a good point. With one hand he grabbed the boy by his scruff and dragged him over the back of his horse. He jumped up and rode for ten minutes beyond the village and into the woodland. There he pushed the lad to the floor, jumped down, and placed the barrel of the gun to the lad's head.

'Now there is no one but you and me.' He cocked the gun. He felt the lad shake. Christian just wanted him to say it was Sir Thomas Ellerby and he would have the man, even if he had to go to the next county to get a decent magistrate to bring him down.

'It was Timothy Squires!' The lad

held his head in his hands.

Christian stepped away and got back on the horse, shaken. He knew Squires was a sheep rustler and had creamed money off his tenants, but to attack them — try to kill them in cold blood — that took an evil mind. His own tenant! He had returned here wanting to find a home, peace and a new start. He had found Ellie; every cloud had a silver lining, Bill would say. Ellie was pure gold. But Christian was going to see justice done. Now he knew who the coward was, he would check on Bill, for he knew that Squires was going nowhere fast. If he thought he had got away with it, he would carry on his life as normal.

'You're not going to shoot me?' the lad asked as he got to his feet, looking at Christian with relief.

'Never was,' Christian said, as he held an arm out for the lad to climb up on the horse behind him. 'I don't shoot boys. But you cannot stand by and watch an attack upon an innocent man and not do or say something — unless you are a coward.'

The lad wiped his eyes with the back of his sleeve.

'He will, he'll wait and he'll beat me to a pulp and leave me in the bog up on the moor. He told me so, and I believe him, for that was how Ned disappeared, and he ... ' He looked away, lips clenched shut as if he had already said too much.

'Who was Ned?' Christian wondered if the man was already a murderer as well as a thief.

'His dog, it went deaf, but it was still a good dog ... ' The lad was struggling not to blubber.

Christian felt a flood of relief, but he could see the pain in the lad's face.

'Do you want a ride home?' Christian asked.

He shook his head. 'No, it wouldn't do to be seen with you. I'll walk back from here.'

'Where is home, lad?' Christian asked.

'Bell Cottage,' he said.

'You're a Mannish?' Christian asked, realising that the lad's father was about to be arrested for sheep rustling too.

The lad nodded.

'Well, our paths will cross again, and soon.' Christian held the reins firmly. What a mess this was turning into.

'Squires threatened Pa with eviction, you know. I have four sisters and a sickly ma,' the lad said before Christian turned the horse to return to the road again.

'Does he profit from the estate's losses?' Christian asked. 'Your pa?'

The lad shook his head. 'Only by keeping the cottage in good order, the land fertile and his sheep pen open for Squires' use.'

'What is your name?' Christian asked, realising the boy was trying to clear his father from any willing involvement with Squires' actions.

'Dan, sir,' The lad walked to the side of the horse.

'Then say nothing, Dan. Not to your pa or anyone. You were not there; you

180

saw nothing and never spoke to me. If your father is a good man, then I will not see harm done to him, or your family, but Squires will fall.'

The lad nodded, and Christian returned to Gorebeck and to Bill. He arrived as Doctor Hughes did; they walked into the room where Bill slept. It was eerily quiet.

★   ★   ★

'Miss Eleanor . . . ' The troubled voice of Mrs Hitchins burst into the morning room as Eleanor finished her breakfast, alone. Christian had not appeared. His place setting lay undisturbed.

'Whatever is it? Mrs Hitchins, you look quite pale!' Eleanor stood up and met the woman as she entered the room.

'Minerve has just told me, that the dairy man told her, that they were attacked last night.' The woman was clearly babbling as she was in some kind of shock.

Eleanor looked at her. 'Calmly now, Mrs Hitchins, who would attack the dairy farmers — or do you mean the cows?' Eleanor's mind was in a spin. Where on earth was Christian? If there was trouble of this nature on the estate, then she needed him there. Disputes, she could sort out; but violence of any kind needed Christian, Squires' or Bill's presence.

'No, Miss Eleanor; Sir and Bill, they were attacked and are still in the town . . . Doctor Hughes was sent for.'

'Goodness! Are they badly hurt? We must go to them and see. Has the doctor been in attendance for both of them?' Eleanor was rushing out of the room. 'Annie, Florrie, one of you fetch my pelisse and get word to Squires that we need the carriage. He will have to come and take us.'

'Yes, we shall both go, Miss Eleanor. I think he just saw Bill. He is tough; he will be fine, won't he?' Mrs Hitchins was hesitating to leave. What on earth was she fussing about Bill for when

Christian could have been struck down, and in goodness knew what condition?

'Yes, yes, of course,' Eleanor snapped. 'Now send young Jeremiah to find Squires urgently — we need the carriage now!'

'Yes, yes, of course.' Mrs Hitchins scurried down to the kitchen as Eleanor quickly dressed for the journey, hoping and praying that Christian was alright. Bill was as tough as old nails, but Christian was a gentleman — her gentleman — he was brave but not so hardy. She stepped outside the Hall and waited as she saw Jeremiah riding back towards the house with Squires.

'Miss Eleanor, do you know what happened, ma'am?' he said as he rode up in front of her. She looked down slightly on him, as the four steps leading to the Hall's entrance placed her above his head height. The man was rugged, although he dressed in a coat of good hardy cloth and wore a robust broad-brimmed hat that shielded his eyes from the autumnal sun, and also from her.

'No, Squires, that is why I need the coach. Please hurry things along. Mrs Hitchins and I need to find out what has occurred. All I know is that they were attacked in Gorebeck and now are at the Hare and Rabbit. We must make haste!'

'Yes, miss, of course.' He kicked the horse so that it cantered around into the yard.

'Thank goodness,' Eleanor said. For in the absence of Christian and his man, at least she had a loyal servant who she could rely on to take her to town. Squires knew the estate and neighbouring ones well as he had been born on one of them; she forgot which one. He had come to work for Howard when their father died and to help out. Her mother's failing health had placed an extra burden upon Howard's shoulders as he took over the running of the estate. So he would know what to do about summoning Charles Dewsbury, the local magistrate, if it had not been done already. Why they should have been attacked bemused Eleanor. It was not like they were connected with the milling industry that had caused such uproar in other parts of the county and beyond. What was the world coming to? This was supposed to be a time of peace — war had ended. Yet there was so much uncertainty and unrest in the country.

Once the coach appeared, Mrs Hitchins stepped outside the Hall, with Minnie waving them off.

Squires pulled on the brake and stepped down gingerly from the front plate. He smiled quickly as he saw Eleanor's look of concern. 'Just a stitch in my side, miss. I came over here a bit quick like, when I heard the news.' He opened the carriage door for them.

'You don't need to worry none. Mr Christian and Bill are soldiers, miss, they'll be fine,' Minnie shouted down to them from the Hall's doorway. 'Take good care of them, Thomas,' she added.

'Of course, Mrs Jennings, or my

name's not Thomas Squires!' he said, and winked up at the cook as Eleanor and Mrs Hitchins took their seats inside.

The coach lurched forward, and Eleanor realised just how distraught Mrs Hitchins was.

'You really care for Bill that much?' she asked, amazed that whilst she had been growing in affection for Christian, her housekeeper had been becoming attached to his man. It was the only explanation for why her housekeeper would be so shaken up by the thought of Bill being hurt. Her own feelings of panic at the thought of Christian being taken from her when she had just discovered how much she cared for him threatened to spill over also. She swallowed and took hold of Mrs Hitchins' hand. 'Oh, what a pair we are, and we have no idea if they are badly hurt or not. We must be strong, Gertrude!'

The woman smiled at Eleanor's use of her Christian name. 'Bill has not yet woken up since he was struck on the back of the head, Miss Eleanor. I found that bit out from the stable lad who had met someone from town when he was out exercising one of the animals early this morning.'

'Oh dear. But a good sleep and he should be fine. What of Christian?' Eleanor asked, and braced herself lest she knew something equally worrying about him.

'He was not hurt. Sir has stayed with Bill. Oh, how worried about Bill he must be! Why, Miss Eleanor, is it that happiness has been waved in my path once more, only to be beaten away by fate again?' The woman sniffed.

Eleanor let go of her hand. 'He is not dead, Mrs Hitchins; compose yourself, please. I will see he has the very best of care.' Eleanor did not mean to sound harsh, but she could not have her crumble in the coach. They needed to have clear heads.

'Yes, yes, of course, forgive me. I speak out of turn . . . ' Mrs Hitchins voice broke.

'No, Mrs Hitchins, you speak out of love. Something we all need, and sometimes have without even realising it, until the threat of its removal is waved before us . . . ' Eleanor blinked away tears.

'Then perhaps we shall both have our chance of happiness restored,' Mrs Hitchins said, and smiled, broader than Eleanor had ever seen the woman do so before.

How lonely a life Mrs Hitchins had had, Eleanor thought. She promised herself in that moment that if God permitted Bill to live, and Christian to forgive her high-handedness when he offered to marry her, that she would accept him at the first opportunity, and see that Mrs Hitchins and Bill also had that same chance if they wished it.

But who would do such a thing? Sir Thomas Ellerby hated Christian, but he was no street brawler. Something niggled at the back of her mind. She needed to see Christian and find out what had actually happened before

188

blaming innocent parties.

They crossed the old bridge by the Norman church and turned towards the Hare and Rabbit. Very soon she would have her answers and all would be well.

13

The coach pulled up alongside the inn.
Mrs Hitchins was so keen to go inside
that she opened the door before the
brake was applied fully and nearly
slipped off the seat.

'Gertrude!' Eleanor shook her head;
the woman was like a lovesick child.

'Sorry,' Mrs Hitchins said and sat
back on the cushion, her hands
gripping each other on her lap.

Squires appeared at the door and
opened it for them. 'Let me find the
stable lad, and then I'll go in and find
out what the situation is, miss,' he said.
He looked surprised when Eleanor
stepped out of the carriage, shortly
followed by Mrs Hitchins.

'You stay with the coach, Squires. We
shall go in and ask for the stable lad to
be sent around to you, and then you
can enter. I have no wish to be left in an

unattended coach.' She walked towards the door, noticing that although Squires nodded, he looked far from pleased.

Eleanor took a moment for her eyes to adjust to the dim light within the inn. She avoided the tap room and headed for the newly created reception area that led to the modern dining room and the newer part of the hotel.

'Can I help you, miss?' a soldier in the smart uniform of the local Yeomanry asked. Unlike the soldiers who had returned in battered and patched-together worn outfits, the local Yeomanry had a fine livery of blue and grey with white brocade on their officers' jackets. He carried his shako under his arm with pride.

'Yes, please. We are looking for Sir Leigh-Bolton and his man Bill.' Eleanor realised that she had never known or used Bill's surname. How strange things had been since Howard and Jemima parted. Lines were being blurred, and yet she no longer cared. She just wanted her home back — and now, she realised, Christian too.

'Ah, yes, I too have been sent to see them.' He looked at Mrs Hitchins, who quickly stepped forward.

'Are they well? Will they live?' she asked, and Eleanor cast her an amazed glance. The woman would have a faint if she kept this up.

'Yes, Mrs . . . '

'Mrs Hitchins,' she added.

'Yes, Mrs Hitchins, they are both alive. Dr. Hughes informed me that Sir Leigh-Bolton has a bruised shoulder, but is fine, and his ex-sergeant breathes more evenly, but will have one nasty headache when he regains consciousness.' He smiled reassuringly back at them. 'Please come with me. I shall take you to Sir Leigh-Bolton and he can answer your questions directly. You are Miss Richards, I take it?' he addressed Eleanor.

'Yes,' she said as she followed him up a flight of stairs to a recently carpeted corridor.

'Then you have saved my man a

journey to Kinsley Hall, for we were asked to convey a message to you that all would be well.' He stopped at a door. 'If you would wait here a moment, I will ask if it is suitable for ladies to enter, or if Sir Leigh-Bolton will see you downstairs in the lounge area. Forgive me if I have brought you up here for no reason.'

'You are forgiven,' Eleanor said.

The man slipped inside the room. 'Well!' Mrs Hitchins said, 'Who does he think he is?'

'The captain of the local Yeomanry!' Eleanor said quietly, 'And you are a housekeeper and a lady, so it is right that we should not burst into a man's bedchamber in an inn, isn't it?'

'I suppose so, but Bill could be . . . '

'Hitchins!' Eleanor snapped, and the woman started but nodded and composed herself again.

Eleanor listened with her ear to the door.

'Captain, I am so glad you have arrived,' Christian was saying.

'I am not the only one, sir. Miss Eleanor and her woman have also come here, seemingly very concerned for the safety of you both.'

'Really! Wonderful — that will save you some time, and guarantees they are kept safe. I will see them in a moment. I need you to take men and arrest my groundsman, Thomas Squires. He attacked us last night.' Christian coughed.

'You have proof that it was this man? You saw him?' The captain looked doubtfully down at a very disorientated Bill on the bed who had clearly been hit from behind.

'No, I was not a witness as such; but you get the man, and you will see he has an injury to his side where I winged him with a bullet from my pistol,' Christian explained.

'Where will I find this man? How do you know he has not gone to ground already?' the captain said, and then added, 'No pun intended, sir.'

'This is no laughing matter. I do not

194

know, but you will have to find him before he does.'

'He is here!' Eleanor burst in. She cared not if they knew she had eavesdropped. This all made sense now. Squires did not have a stitch in his side: he had a wound. 'He brought us in the coach, Christian.'

'Then we have him!' Christian said, but as they spoke a horse was heard galloping away from outside the inn. Dan was staggering out of the stable, holding the side of his face.

'Damn him!' Christian said as he stared out of the window.

'We'll find him, don't worry, sir,' the captain said, and left the room in great haste. Mrs Hitchins went straight to Bill's side. The man looked up and half-smiled, grimaced at the effort of moving his head and closed his eyes again.

'Mrs Hitchins, would you stay and see he is kept safe?' Christian asked.

'Of course,' she said, and pulled over a chair to sit by the man's bedside.

Christian walked over to Eleanor and stepped outside the room. In the privacy of the corridor he kissed her tenderly on her welcoming lips, but then stood straight.

'Christian, I was so worried for you!' She lifted on tiptoe and kissed his lips.

He flinched as her hand pressed on his shoulder to raise herself higher. Instantly she stepped back.

'It's only a bruise,' he said dismissively.

'Will Bill be alright?' she asked.

'Yes, but for a few hours I was frightened I had lost him, Ellie. That on top of the thought of losing you too, for you are so against accepting my proposal, it was almost too much to bear. I thought we could have a loving future together as man and wife. You may not love me now, but in marriages that are arranged, this can grow afterwards — can't it?' He cast his eyes down as if ashamed of his entreaty.

'I never said that I did not love you. Neither did I reject you. That I will never do, Christian. I was just too proud and blind to admit it. Fate has brought us together, and . . . ' She fell silent.

'What is it?' Christian saw a look of realisation dawn upon her face as she stopped speaking.

'Christian, I believe Sir Thomas Ellerby is behind this attack. He hates you, despises me for not taking up his friend's offer and living under your roof instead. He is also owed money by Howard, or was.' Eleanor was quite certain she had sorted out the problem.

'I thought so too, but it was definitely Squires who attacked us, and there is no connection between them that I know of.' He stroked her cheek gently with his hand and she leaned into it.

'Yes, there is. You see Squires was raised on his estate. He was sent over here to help Howard run the tenancies, for he had no notion of how the estate worked, and Thomas offered Squires as a good man of excellent character and knowledge. He seemed so efficient, and Howard trusted him.'

'Then if the man goes to ground now, in panic, he will return to his master. You must stay here with Mrs Hitchins and I will sort this mess out with the captain. They will be looking on the wrong estate.'

'No . . . I . . . '

'Yes, because if Bill awakens properly, it will take the two of you to hold him down and prevent him trying to come after me . . . Promise?' He was holding both of her shoulders and looking straight into her worried eyes.

'Very well, Christian. But stay safe.'

He kissed her full on her mouth, lingering a delicious moment, which was only cut short when voices were heard on the stairs. He pulled away, opened the bedchamber door and bustled her inside, closing it quickly before they could be seen together.

★ ★ ★

Eleanor arranged for broth to be sent to Bill's room for the three of them, although she sat by the window overlooking the street waiting for any sign of a return by Christian.

Mrs Hitchins spooned delicate mouthfuls of the broth into Bill's mouth after the two of them managed to prop him up on a bolster pillow. His colour, initially drained, gradually came back to him, as did a smile.

Once his wits seemed to return fully to him, Eleanor could see the light of love flicker in his eyes as they mirrored Mrs Hitchins'. She felt a little awkward, and was tempted to leave them alone; but being in an inn — even a respectable one — on her own, she dared not.

It was hours later that Christian finally returned to her. The door opened and the cold air wafted into the room with him.

'Thought you'd abandoned me in heaven,' Bill quipped as he looked from one woman to the other.

'Good to see you looking chipper, Bill. How's the head?' Christian asked as he walked over to Eleanor, who was seated by the window.

'It's been better, but I am a hard nut to crack. Did you find the b — . . . blighter?' Bill asked, his eyes fixed on Christian's face.

'Squires is now in the lock-up. We took him all the way down to York — save the local magistrate from the hassle of judging him.' He winked, knowing Squires had friends who would help him escape given half a chance if he was kept in Gorebeck. 'I have set all the charges and he will languish there until the next assizes.'

Bill half-smiled his approval. He obviously could not shake his head or nod.

'Did you have Sir Thomas arrested too?' Eleanor asked, looking up into Christian's tired eyes.

'No proof would stick to him, despite the dirt that encases his good name. We only have the accusations of a liar and a thief — Squires, if he admits it. Chances are, he would rely on Thomas and his friends to find a way of getting him out.' Christian shrugged and sat down next to Eleanor, holding her hand in his.

'Then he walks away and can try to hurt you again,' she said.

'No, that he will not. For, you see, he has been summoned to pay a debt of £1578 3s 7d by tomorrow night, which he cannot pay. So he will be escorted to debtors' prison tomorrow, and his wife to her sister's in Hastings. I have arranged transport for her. The estate will be sold.' Christian smiled. 'I own the man's debts, you see. He may be able to evade the law on many things, protected by privilege and his magistrate friend Charles Hughes, but a called-in debt — or, in his case, debts — cannot be escaped so easily.'

Eleanor hugged him, and Bill raised his eyebrows at Mrs Hitchins, who surprised him by kissing his cheek ever so quickly. He squeezed her hand.

'When can we go home?' Bill asked.

Christian smiled. 'We all return to Kinsley Hall this night.'

'Come, Eleanor, we shall have the coach made ready. It is time our family was settled into the Hall. Bill, I have a need for a good estate manager and groundsman. It is a position that comes with a new to-be-built cottage on the estate. You are welcome to live in Kinsley until then, where Mrs Hitchins can oversee your full recovery.'

The woman blushed.

Bill chuckled. 'Sounds good to me,' he said.

'Come down when you are both ready. We will be in the lounge.' Eleanor and Christian left.

★ ★ ★

Before they left the corridor, Christian swept Eleanor into his arms. 'Now, answer me, woman, without interruption.' He fell to his knee, still holding her hands, 'Will you be my wife?'

202

Eleanor chuckled and knelt in front of him. 'Yes!' she said, and they embraced as if they would never part, but did when a startled captain appeared at the top of the staircase. He coughed, and both stood, holding hands and laughing.

'Be the first to congratulate me, captain! We are to wed,' Eleanor said, and the man shook Christian's hand in congratulation before Christian and Eleanor stepped out into the world together — her heart and home secure.

We do hope that you have enjoyed reading this large print book.

Did you know that all of our titles are available for purchase?

We publish a wide range of high quality large print books including:
Romances, Mysteries, Classics
General Fiction
Non Fiction and Westerns

Special interest titles available in large print are:
The Little Oxford Dictionary
Music Book, Song Book
Hymn Book, Service Book

Also available from us courtesy of Oxford University Press:
Young Readers' Dictionary
(large print edition)
Young Readers' Thesaurus
(large print edition)

For further information or a free brochure, please contact us at:
Ulverscroft Large Print Books Ltd.,
The Green, Bradgate Road, Anstey,
Leicester, LE7 7FU, England.
Tel: (00 44) 0116 236 4325
Fax: (00 44) 0116 234 0205

NEW YEAR, NEW GUY

Angela Britnell

When Polly organises a surprise reunion for her fiancé and his long-lost American friend, her sister, Laura, grudgingly agrees to help keep the secret. And when the plain-spoken, larger-than-life Hunter McQueen steps off the bus in her rainy Devon town and only just squeezes into her tiny car, it confirms that Laura has made a big mistake in going along with her sister's crazy plan. But could the tall, handsome man with the Nashville drawl be just what Laura needs to shake up her life and start something new?

THE GHOST IN THE WINDOW

Cara Cooper

Working on a forthcoming movie, Siobhan Frost travels to a beautiful French chateau run by the charismatic Christian Lavelle. Having taken the job to escape her failed engagement, she is shocked when her ex, Gerrard, turns up. And when Philadelphia, the starlet appearing in the film, makes eyes at Gerrard, Siobhan is left in turmoil. One thing is for sure — the chateau has secrets and Christian is determined to solve them with Siobhan's help.

IT STARTED WITH A GIGGLE

Kirsty Kerry

On a night out in Edinburgh, single mum Liza-Belle Graham finds herself revealing her hopes and dreams to a green-eyed stranger. Liza has always wanted to run an 'arty-crafty-booky' business, and she's seen the perfect empty shop . . . But Scott McCreadie is an interior designer looking for new premises. And when Liza arranges a viewing she bumps into none other than Scott trying to steal her perfect shop! Is Liza's dream in jeopardy, or is a new dream about to begin?

FEARLESS HEART

Dawn Knox

Whilst serving at RAF Holsmere, Genevieve longs to contribute more to the war effort. With her knowledge of France and its language, and her love of action, she joins the Special Operations Executive as a French agent. However, once in France, Genevieve realises she must be braver and tougher than her male counterparts before they'll accept her. Gradually, she achieves their respect but will she ever win over Yves, the man whose love she yearns for?